To my ever-patient wife, Ruth.

Acknowledgements and thanks

In 2014, I prompted my daughter Heidi to write a Bible-based story. Her response was that I should show her how! This is my attempt to do so.

Particular thanks go to Ruth, my wife, who helped me find time to write, patiently read what I wrote, and humoured me when I spent inordinate amounts of time on research into minute details.

Feedback from early readers and subscribers has improved the story greatly, so I thank them. No manuscript is ever without errors, but these early readers helped eliminate most typos, bad grammar and uncomfortable usage. Cathy, my oldest daughter has tirelessly undertaken the thankless task of proof reading the entire manuscript more than once. Thanks, Cathy.

My son Chris has also helped with various technical details and his excellent reading has made the audio book a pleasure to listen to. I never expected to enjoy listening to anything I had written, but Chris achieved this.

A request

I have a request to make of all readers: if you find any errors; typos, spelling errors, poor grammar, unkempt use of vocabulary, or, most importantly, errors of fact where the story misrepresents the Bible, please let me know. I can't correct printed books, but electronic versions and any new printed editions can be fixed.

Terror on Every Side!

THE LIFE OF JEREMIAH

VOLUME 3 – Darkness Falling

Mark Morgan

ISBN (eBook): 978-1-925587-12-8
ISBN (Paperback): 978-1-925587-02-9

Bible
Tales
www.BibleTales.online

Cover picture: Jerusalem from the Mount of Olives
by Frederick Edwin Church (1870).

Free Download

Paul in Snippets

A 109-page PDF novelette by Mark Morgan.

The life of Paul painted from the Acts of the Apostles.

Get your free copy of *Paul in Snippets* when you sign up for the Bible Tales mailing list. As well as the eBook, you will receive a weekly email newsletter with micro tales, informative articles and special offers.

Visit **http://www.BibleTales.online/free-pins**

VOLUME THREE

Darkness Falling

Contents

"Terror on Every Side!"

For I hear the whispering of many—
terror on every side!—
as they scheme together against me,
as they plot to take my life.

A psalm of David: Psalm 31:13

For I hear many whispering.
Terror is on every side!
"Denounce him! Let us denounce him!"
say all my close friends,
watching for my fall.
"Perhaps he will be deceived;
then we can overcome him
and take our revenge on him."

Jeremiah 20:10

Chapter 1

The High Priest

April, 619 BC – the 20th year of King Josiah

My father sort of faded away.

I am reconciled to his death, but I can never really be satisfied with all the missed opportunities. From an early age, one looks up to one's parents, and a son should honour and admire his father. My father was admired by all and was a master at keeping the peace, particularly with idolaters and pagans. His voice could woo enemies and friends alike. To hear him read the scriptures – when I was young, before his eyesight began to fail – was pure pleasure.

Two years before, in the eighteenth year of Josiah, when I returned to Judah after the discovery of the Book of the Law in the temple, I had noticed a little shakiness, a little caution in his step, a few signs of old age. His fall that night on the road to Anathoth had been the start of a gradual decline. He had never been able to walk easily after that and had lived in the High Priest's house in Jerusalem from then until his death. His eyesight had continued to worsen so that he could no longer read or even see very well, and his voice had begun to fail too. Increasingly, he had seemed to be sick with a cold, and he had begun to feel pain in his legs all the time. His pain was worst during the cold weather, and my mother had been rightly worried about him during his last winter. He had spent most of the time in bed. Shortly after the Passover, he had again got a cold; then one day about a week later, as he was talking to my mother, he had suddenly stopped, clutched at his chest and then never spoke again. Before nightfall, he was dead, and the sad tidings had been carried to the king and to my brother Azariah.

I heard the shocking news the next morning from the servant Azariah sent to convey the information. With my mother and father living in Jerusalem, I had been living alone in our house in Anathoth for most of the time when I was in Judah. Azariah and I walked to Jerusalem together that morning, and I think we were both in shock. For me, it had come as a big surprise and I felt a great sense of loss, despite the fact that my father and I had had many arguments over the seven years that had passed since that memorable night of my seventeenth birthday. For Azariah, though, there would be not only a sense of loss, but also a suddenly increased responsibility. The spiritual weight of a nation had fallen on his shoulders and he must bear it without any advice from his father.

We walked in silence for much of the way, and I wondered what the future would bring between us. The future had suddenly come much closer, and now my work as a prophet must involve interacting with a new High Priest to deliver a message of coming destruction which was now seven years closer than it had been when I had first experienced the voice of Yahweh. Azariah and I had never got on well – he viewed me as an upstart idealist with a blinkered view of life, while I considered him to be sadly detached from the God he worshipped, more interested in the mode and means of worship than in the God who inspired our worship. The confrontations of the past could now easily become more common – and more bitter.

The day was a typical spring morning in Anathoth, sunny and warming quickly. Flocks of travelling birds still flew uncaring overhead, and Anathoth, perched on its unremarkable hill, remained as testament to the fact that life goes on, though the protagonists change. Roads recently mended after a cold, wet winter still carried people into and out of this unimportant village inhabited mostly by priests and Levites. Yet one of its more important sons had left its streets never to return. Israel's leader of worship had finished his course. His work had been left to another, one of the next generation – a generation which would make its peace with God, or not, as it chose. My father's work was done, but his legacy would live on in the Book of the Law of God that he had uncovered in the temple. The copies made under his supervision could guide the worship of the nation through generations to come, but we who outlived him would choose how important it was. Azariah was to be the new hand guiding the worship of the people of God. It seemed like a big change – one of the biggest changes of my life – yet around me the world continued unaffected.

❧

A little more than two years had elapsed between the great Passover of King Josiah and the death of my father, and I had spent much of that time in other nations. I had seen the Nile River and delivered a message to Pharaoh, which had taken my very best efforts and the blessings of God to achieve. I had even crossed the Euphrates River and visited some smaller kingdoms in the north. Three times in each year, I had returned to Jerusalem to keep the feasts which God had commanded all Israelite men to attend in Jerusalem.

Throughout that time, King Josiah had kept his direction and maintained his enthusiasm for the God of his fathers, but the work of leading a nation had taken its toll on him. Urgent reformation is admirable and inspiring, but the ongoing task of reshaping attitude and driving constant religious renewal is far more trying. Josiah's faith still shone in everything he did, but his proselytising zeal had been overshadowed by the urgent but mundane matters of ruling a kingdom. Never again would he ride at the head of a column of men burning with the desire to purge Judah of her thanklessness and unfaithfulness. Already, the paroxysm of purity was exhausted and any remaining energy was directed towards trying to hold on to the advantage gained.

For the moment, the enemies of the worship of Yahweh had quietly withdrawn, hiding themselves under an appearance of godliness, concealing their true colours, continuing to attend feasts and display a habit of acceptable expression. But God was never the object of their love within either their homes or their minds.

Already, the best had passed. Looking back past the horror of the sickening downward spiral presided over by Josiah's sons, it is easy to delineate the bright summer of Josiah's reign, a season of inspirational leadership; but it is also easy to see where midsummer passed and the relentless descent into winter began.

Josiah had made a mighty effort – and he never gave up. His lifelong struggle against Manasseh's legacy was monumental, but it was a failure. He might just as well have tried to stop the incoming tide. Too many people find evil delightful and constraint unacceptable.

Let me also provide what balance I can. Though Josiah's tireless work failed to save the nation, it did help individuals. Shobai, Miriam, Maacah and their friends from Bethel were all helped enormously by Josiah's visits to Israel and by the first Passover he commanded. They had already been determined in their faith, but Josiah had added the support of authority, which makes goodness easier. Josiah made it easier for his subjects to choose God, and some took the opportunity. Zaccai and Abigail, with whom Shobai and the others had stayed during that first Passover, were led to a closer worship of Yahweh by Josiah. In the lives of these individuals and others like them, Josiah won. A king must rule for his entire nation, but sometimes the real benefits of his work go to only a select few.

Josiah's true success was seen in the lives of those who chose to follow Yahweh and passed on their love of God to their children. Some of those children would later go into captivity and die in a foreign land, longing for the land of their fathers – but they would die in faith.

This diary is taking much longer to write than I ever expected it to. I began it in frustration on the evening after Johanan accused me of not speaking the words of God and not being sent by Yahweh. Thinking back over the years stirs up all sorts of memories, both good and bad. The ones that fill me with joy are the memories of the responses of individuals who saw God's offer of life and reached out for it. These were the wonderful long-term results of Josiah's work, and I hope to write more about some of them later – if I live long enough.

❧

Azariah and I arrived in Jerusalem; two walking together, but each wrapped up in his own thoughts. For the next seven days, Azariah's time would be dedicated to his ordination as High Priest. As High Priest, he was not permitted to make himself unclean through contact with any dead body, not even that of his father.[1] Personal wishes and opinions must be subjugated to his task of representing his nation before God. For the High Priest, holiness must come first. In some ways, my position as a prophet was similar: my freedom was limited by the commands of God, which made my life a living parable to those around me. Others were permitted to marry and welcome children as a heritage of Yahweh, but I must not. Others could celebrate happy events and mourn sad ones, but I had not this freedom.[2]

After entering the city through the Benjamin gate, we made our way to the house of the High Priest, now a house of mourning. Neither of us could enter, but each wished to leave a message of sympathy and condolence for our mother. A servant greeted us and we each wrote a brief note on a small piece of papyrus, requesting that they be delivered as soon as possible.

Our mother would not expect either of us to go into the house, as she knew both Azariah's position and the constraints that God had placed upon me. We had discussed these constraints shortly after Josiah's great Passover when she had asked me my intentions regarding Maacah, whom she had liked at first sight. She had noticed that I had largely withdrawn from any interaction with Maacah over the last couple of days of the feast and had wanted to know why. I had explained God's command against marriage, which had come as such a shock to me, and also the limitations on both mourning and celebrations. Disappointment had brought tears to her eyes as, once again, she had been quicker than I to see the ramifications of these commands. She pointed out that our relatives, already unhappy with my work as a

---

[1] Leviticus 21:10-12
[2] Jeremiah 16:5, 8

prophet, would be sure to respond with criticism and anger when I did not join them in mourning the next death in the family.

She had been right. Soon after the end of the Feast of Unleavened Bread in the eighteenth year of King Josiah, Gemariah's sickly young son, Hasshub, died. I had explained God's instructions to Gemariah, but though he had said that he accepted the situation, he still implied that I had let him down. Gemariah and Abigail had both been understandably upset about their loss, and my inability to share in their mourning had done nothing to assuage their grief.

℞

After leaving our messages at the house, Azariah and I went directly to the temple and found messengers from the king and several priests waiting. Of course, they weren't waiting for me, but for once, Azariah seemed happy that I was there.

Zechariah and Jehiel, the two most senior remaining priests, welcomed us.

"Azariah and Jeremiah, we have been terribly saddened by the death of your father, although it was not completely unexpected," said Zechariah, gently.

I remember feeling surprised at his words – my father's death *had* been completely unexpected to me.

"So now, Azariah," continued Jehiel, "we must appoint a new High Priest, and, based on our advice, King Josiah has suggested that you are the right person for this responsibility."

"Are you willing to be ordained for this task which your father carried out so faithfully before you?" asked Zechariah.

Azariah looked down, his face working as he struggled to control his emotions. Finally, he nodded, very slowly.

Zechariah put his hand on Azariah's shoulder in sympathy and I struggled to stem my own tears.

Achbor the son of Micaiah was the leader of the king's representatives, and Zechariah looked to him for confirmation, receiving a silent nod of assent. Zechariah turned and said to Azariah, "Israel cannot be without a High Priest. Your nation needs you now. Are you ready?"

Without speaking, my brother nodded again, and Zechariah repeated the instructions God had given to Moses before ever the tabernacle was made or the clothes of the priests tailored:

> "The holy garments of Aaron shall be for his sons after him; they shall be anointed in them and ordained in them. The son who succeeds him as priest, who comes into the temple to minister in the Holy Place, shall wear them seven days."[3]

Then Zechariah led him towards a doorway where a few junior priests stood waiting. The door was opened and Zechariah ushered my brother through it into another room to prepare for the ceremony.

While we waited outside, Azariah washed himself with water and was then solemnly dressed in the clothes of his new position. For the rest of his life, these clothes would be a constant reminder that he was one of the people, yet not one of them. As High Priest, he must first represent, serve and obey God, honouring him before the nation. As one of the people of Israel, he must be understanding and encouraging, acknowledging failure and seeking national forgiveness while doing his best to inspire an ongoing growth in godliness. For a few moments, I wondered how it would feel to be in his

---

[3] Exodus 29:29-30, slightly modified

position – the one person in the nation who could carry the sins of the nation before the Most High God in search of forgiveness for the people. The task seemed overwhelming, and I felt glad that God had given me only the task of being a prophet. Was it ironic that God had forbidden me to pray for my people when my brother must be High Priest for the nation? How I hoped that he would be inspired to see the importance of his work and to realise how much depended on his humble worship of God.

As we waited, Jehiel went out of the room, returning soon afterwards with several priests and Levites who were known for their skill and interest in music. One of these was Meshullam, whom I knew from our involvement with the reviewing of the Book of the Law of God two years before.

After a time, the door opened again and Azariah was led back into the room. His clothes had been designed by God for glory and for beauty[4] and he certainly made a striking figure, from the turban with its golden plate down to the alternating bells and pomegranates which hung from the hem of his blue robe and tinkled as he walked to the centre of the room.

A table stood in one corner of the room, and Jehiel took from it a small container, filled with specially prepared anointing oil.[5] Silently, he walked to where Azariah stood waiting. My brother had obviously been instructed what to do, as he bent forwards slightly, inclining his head towards Jehiel and slipping the turban towards the back of his head. This left the front of his head and hair uncovered. Slowly, Jehiel poured the oil from the container and a golden stream ran down onto Azariah's head, coursing through his hair and across his

---

[4] Exodus 28:2, 40
[5] Exodus 30:22-33

forehead and cheeks, then slowly running down his beard and dripping unevenly to the floor, where it gathered in small clear puddles.

As Azariah still stood silently, Zechariah intoned the words that Moses had spoken to Aaron when Aaron and his sons were being ordained, altered slightly to reflect the fact that Solomon had built a temple of stone and cedar to replace the tent of meeting that had travelled with Israel through the wilderness:

> "Do not let the hair of your head hang loose, and do not tear your clothes, lest you die, and wrath come upon all the congregation. And do not go outside the entrance of the temple, lest you die, for the anointing oil of the Lord is upon you."[6]

> "Drink no wine or strong drink when you go into the house of God, lest you die. You are to distinguish between the holy and the common, and between the unclean and the clean, and you are to teach the people of Israel all the statutes that the Lord has spoken to them by Moses."[7]

The priests and Levites sang some of the words of King David:

> "Praise the Lord!
> Oh give thanks to the Lord, for he is good,
> for his steadfast love endures forever!
> Who can utter the mighty deeds of the Lord,
> or declare all his praise?
> Blessed are they who observe justice,
> who do righteousness at all times!
> Remember me, O Lord, when you show favour
> to your people; help me when you save them,
> that I may look upon the prosperity of your chosen ones,

---

[6] from Leviticus 10:6-7, slightly modified
[7] Leviticus 10:9-11, slightly modified

that I may rejoice in the gladness of your nation,
    that I may glory with your inheritance."[8]

For the next seven days, Azariah would have to stay in a small room at the entrance to the temple. During that entire time, he would continue to wear the clothes of his calling and must not leave the temple for any reason. The specified sacrifices for ordination would all be offered, and on the eighth day, Azariah would be fully ordained, permanently appointed to the position of High Priest to Yahweh, a position he would hold until his death.

On the eighth day of Aaron's period of ordination, God's glory had been shown to all the people and the fire of God had consumed the burnt offering.[9] I remember wondering, as I watched my brother begin the process of ordination that morning, whether God's glory would be revealed in the same way or whether the time of miracles was past forever. Would fire fall from heaven on the altar of God in these modern times? And if it did, would we welcome it as the power of God or wonder who had set up the trick?

Later that morning, my father was buried, carried from the house of the High Priest by Gemariah and five other relatives. I was told that a large crowd followed, with the mourning women wailing loudly and others walking in quiet respect for this priest who was loved for his work for religious unity and tolerance in the nation. His body was placed in a tomb of honour within the walls of Jerusalem – and I could not be there to help.

The new High Priest stayed in the temple of God, isolated by God's rules from the sad but necessary work of burial.

I remember that day as being one of the hardest days of all my service to God as a prophet. Obediently, I kept

---

[8] Psalm 106:1-5
[9] Leviticus 9:22-24

away from the house of mourning and was not one of the party placing my father's body in the tomb – but how I longed to be there, consoling my mother and helping Gemariah in his difficult task of burying the man who had given us life and brought us up in a happy and comfortable home. My obedience won me criticism and disdain, and I wondered whether anyone paid attention to the reason why it must be done. God had said:

"Do not enter the house of mourning,
or go to lament or grieve for them,
for I have taken away my peace from this people,
my steadfast love and mercy, declares the Lord.

"Both great and small shall die in this land.
They shall not be buried,
and no one shall lament for them
or cut himself or make himself bald for them.

"No one shall break bread for the mourner,
to comfort him for the dead,
nor shall anyone give him the cup of consolation
to drink for his father or his mother."[10]

God had commanded my absence to highlight his coming judgement, but no-one wanted to understand it that way. I had tried to explain God's wishes to a few of my relatives, but they had listened with little patience and a curling lip, and maintained their original conclusion: that my absence was a sign of gross filial disrespect and personal animosity.

That day may have been the start of a new phase in my life. Hatred found its way into my family, and I was its target. I knew that my relatives and the townsfolk did not like my message, but I was ignorant of the depths of that feeling against me and was like a gentle lamb being led to the slaughter.

---

[10] Jeremiah 16:5-7

It was not to be long before I knew all about it, but for the time being, I was only aware of the depressing feeling of being unpopular. I wallowed in self-pity.

But there was more to come. I was soon to make another enemy.

Chapter 2

In a narrow lane

"Ow! Stop it! Help! Help!"

The shouts seemed to come from a narrow lane that joined the street I was traversing just a short distance ahead, near the Potsherd Gate in Jerusalem.

Quickly, I ran to the corner as the shouts continued and the cries of pain increased. It was late in the day, and the sun was sinking in the west as I turned the corner and stopped to look around. Dark shadows filled the narrow lane in which I found myself.

"Help! Oh, please stop!" The voice was that of a young lad. His right hand was held firmly in the grip of a slightly older lad who was holding a staff with which he was repeatedly striking the younger boy.

Taking in the scene, I wondered what was going on. Things didn't seem quite right. There were several people standing around watching, but no-one was making any attempt to interfere in the one-sided struggle. The older boy was about fourteen or fifteen years old and dressed in expensive, foreign-looking clothes, while the younger boy was probably about twelve, poorly dressed and considerably smaller.

I hurried to the group and looked around, "What's going on?" I asked.

The lad with the staff ignored me and kept striking, the rod rising and falling brutally.

Leaning against the wall of one of the houses lining the lane was a man who was also dressed in bright-coloured clothes of a foreign cut. He was the only one to respond to my question: "Mind your own business and go away," he said truculently, in a voice that I recognised. It was Asaiah, King Josiah's servant and close associate. Once again his arrogant and aggressive response made me wonder what King Josiah appreciated in him. Surely he must have a better side? – but I had never seen any hint of it.

"Help me! Help me!" the younger boy begged me imploringly as he cringed under the blows.

The request seemed to anger the older lad and he raised his staff high over his head as if to strike an even heavier blow. The end of the staff arced down over his back as his hands reached the highest point of his swing. Seizing the opportunity, I stepped forward and grabbed the staff just as his hands began their downward stroke. He tried to swing the rod up and over his head but was surprised by the unexpected resistance. Stumbling, he lost his balance and fell to the ground at my feet in a flurry of expensive material. The situation reminded me strongly of the time when I had been attacked by a group of idolaters on the path outside Anathoth.

Asaiah frowned at me angrily before stepping forward to help the stick-wielding youth to his feet. "My lord!" he said with concern, brushing the dust off the fine clothes. This was the first sign of anything but anger and contempt that I had ever seen from this man. It was a pleasant change, but what had sparked this concern?

"Who's he and why did he interfere?" the lad asked, pointing a shaking finger at me. There was enough anger in his voice to more than make up for any lack of it in Asaiah's voice.

"That, my prince, is Jeremiah, the son of Hilkiah, a man who cannot keep his hands from meddling in other people's business." Asaiah's voice was recovering its customary overtones.

"Is he the son of Hilkiah, the High Priest who just died?"

"Yes, Eliakim," Asaiah agreed.

"The one you said was no loss?" Eliakim continued in a sneering voice.

"Hold your tongue, prince!" Asaiah said sharply, having the grace to look a little abashed.

Eliakim was King Josiah's oldest son, and I recognised him – now that I knew who he was. It seemed that I was continuing my habit of making powerful enemies. No wonder the rest of the small crowd had been afraid to interfere. Prince Eliakim was expected to be the next king of Judah, and there were already many stories spreading in Jerusalem of his selfishness and uncontrolled violence. As he fell, Eliakim had let go of the young lad whom he had been beating, and the boy had wisely taken the opportunity to scuttle away and hide. Unfortunately, that left me as the only target for his anger.

"Why did you interfere?" he asked. He spoke quietly, but there was a chilling menace in his look and tone that didn't bode well for my future if he ever became king. "Don't you know who I am?"

"I didn't recognise you, my prince, but even if I had, I would still have done the same," I responded. "Why were you beating the lad?"

"He ran into me as I was walking along the lane," Eliakim replied, indignantly. "Playing foolish games – he deserved to be punished." He started to look around for his victim, but the boy had vanished. Suddenly, Eliakim noticed that I was still holding his staff. "Give me my staff," he demanded.

I was in a quandary: should I return the staff and possibly have it used on me by this uncontrolled adolescent? Or should I keep it to teach him a lesson? On the other hand, he was a prince of Judah and the staff was his. It was a difficult decision, but eventually, I gave it back to him with a reminder from the law of Yahweh that God wants us to love our neighbour and that a stick was not a good way to show that love when the boy had just made a simple mistake.

Eliakim snatched the staff from my outstretched hand and snarled at me, "You can keep your religion to yourself. Don't try to tell me what to do."

Asaiah and Eliakim left immediately thereafter, and I was left with a few other bystanders who had stood watching the whole scene without intervening.

Suddenly I started to wonder: why had Asaiah and Eliakim been in this corner of Jerusalem anyway, near the Potsherd Gate and the notorious Valley of the Son of Hinnom? Surely there was nothing in this gloomy lane that could attract a nobleman and the king's son? But as I could imagine no answer to this question, my mind turned back to the conflict I had interrupted.

"Does anyone know where the young lad is?" I enquired, feeling that I should check that he was alright.

One of the bystanders, a middle-aged man, advised me that he would be in the last house in the lane, "The one next to the shrine," he added.

"The shrine?" I repeated, rather taken aback.

"Yes, the shrine of Baal," he replied, "right at the end of the roadway, up against the city wall."

Obviously, the reports I had heard were true: idolatry was indeed making a comeback. Could this be the reason why Asaiah and Eliakim had made their way to this dark laneway?

Chapter 3

Holding fast?

Life in the kingdom of Judah went on. King Josiah was popular and his people did their best to keep him happy.

Since Josiah's courageous destruction of idols and their more horrific forms of worship in his eighteenth year, the public areas of Jerusalem had remained free of idols – although my brush with Eliakim had made me realise that there might be forces working quietly to undermine this situation. Nevertheless, the temple area had been maintained in the glory and beauty David had intended when he imagined and prepared for a house of God.

My father had overseen the work of clearing, cleaning and subsequently maintaining the temple and its courtyards to some extent, but his chief input had been to choose men who would do the work faithfully and well; men like Meshullam, an experienced and gifted Levite who had proved to be excellent at supervising the workmen. With his other skills as a scribe and musician, he was a valuable asset among those who worked in the temple.

The priests of the second rank, chosen for their administrative skills, had also become more important as the temple was visited more widely and my father's health deteriorated. As time passed, they became more and more like a separate hierarchy among the priests, and the work of the temple was effectively split into two areas: worship, and operations and maintenance. The High Priest was still the nominal leader, but he concentrated largely on the organisation of the day to day worship in the temple, while the management of the buildings and the admission and control of the public were looked after by the priests of the second rank.

The study of the law of God had become much more common among the Levites and priests. The newly-discovered Book of the Law of Yahweh had given us all much more confidence regarding the scriptures we had inherited from our forebears. Hundreds of modern scrolls had been acknowledged as fraudulent based on the large numbers of ancient scrolls which all agreed with each other but disagreed with the modern ones. Most of these corrupted scrolls had been destroyed, but some had been kept as reminders after being clearly identified as false. I would have been happier if they had all been destroyed.

Everything about the city looked splendid and the temple was the showcase of a nation which had turned to Yahweh again.

A quick visit to the capital of Judah would have convinced anyone that the nation was dedicated to Yahweh and worshipped him with love. The temple was clean and tidy, busy at times, and always filled with priests and Levites going about the business of worship. Worshippers brought gifts; daily, weekly and monthly sacrifices were performed. Choir practice in the temple was quite an attraction, and the singing of praise to God frequently echoed grandly around. The names of other gods were fading from the national vocabulary, too – at least in public.

Had a visitor come at the time of one of the three annual national feasts, particularly the Passover, he would have seen large crowds of people and felt the serious grandeur of formal worship in the house of Yahweh. He would have seen people rejoicing in their worship and thanking God for his blessings.

This was the outward appearance of things.

Had it not been for the recurring words of God which continued to remind me of coming destruction – and the altar of Baal I had recently seen near the Potsherd Gate – I would probably have been taken in by the appearance too. With that background, however, I was able to see that the city had a private life that was rather different from its public life. The public celebrations of God's feasts presented a nation revelling in the joy of holy worship and thankfulness, but little things gave away the true situation. A concentration on external things hinted that the worship was more for the sake of appearances than as an overflowing of gratitude and praise to a generous and loving creator. The new rules for worship seemed to concentrate on maintaining the sanctity of the temple at all costs, rather than enabling worshippers to meet with God within its walls.

Yahweh, the unseen God, had brought Israel out of Egypt and given us laws which would lead to holiness, happiness and health. King Josiah had inherited a kingdom which ignored these rules, but his personal choice had been to serve God. As king, he had also done the best he could to lead his nation to holiness, to the obedience that would warrant the blessings God had promised.

Practically, all we had to do was to look impartially at the evidence. God had listed blessings and curses:[11] which were we receiving?

Little examination was necessary: life expectancies were low, health was bad, droughts were common, national security was poor, and happiness seemed unattainable except fleetingly through the drunkenness that was so widespread in the nation. King David had lived until he was 70, but no king since had lived that long. Why? In early times, my tribe, the Levites, had walked with God and lived long and satisfying lives. Aaron had left Egypt at 83 to wander the wilderness of Sinai for 40 years before dying at the age of 123. My father had just died at an age that was much younger than Aaron's when he left Egypt. The only example I knew of a priest living a long life in recent times was Jehoiada, who had taken a stand for God against Athaliah and lived to the amazing age of 130 as he protected the young prince Joash! Individual examples can never show everything, but the overall picture was clear: as a nation, we continued to choose ungodliness, and ungodliness was killing us.

Josiah had tried to turn his nation back to God and had taken strong steps to do his best to achieve it, as directed by the Book of the Law of Yahweh.

People had worshipped idols, so Josiah had destroyed their idols and encouraged the nation to worship Yahweh. But instead, they had turned to worshipping the temple.

Corrupt and evil behaviour had filled the life of the nation, so Josiah had encouraged them to follow the commands in the Book of the Law, with its frequent references to holiness and godliness. Instead, people had pursued an appearance of holiness; the love for God that should prompt our worship seemed absent.

---

[11] Deuteronomy 27 & 28

The people had agreed to Josiah's request and confirmed the covenant with Yahweh, but had the covenant really found a place in their hearts?

Topheth had been the sordid centre of child sacrifice. Josiah had desecrated it, and in doing so, had saved the God-given lives of thousands of children. However, rumours now suggested that the practice was regaining popularity and that fires burned again in Topheth, hidden from the king's eye. God's gift of life was being thrown away to placate the imagined anger of dead idols. With each such senseless murder, the stench of the land in God's nose increased,[12] and the final destruction of Judah came another irrevocable step closer.

☙

The episode with Eliakim near the Potsherd Gate had brought the question of where the kingdom was headed to the forefront of my mind. Even at a very early age, Josiah's sons had showed no signs of loving God as their father did, but Eliakim's behaviour in the laneway had been frightening. Here was a future king who considered it his right to violently assault a young lad who accidentally knocked against him in the street! Although I had never known Josiah as a young man, I could not imagine any such behaviour from him. Instead, this fitted with what I had heard of Manasseh, and the thought horrified me.

Though Asaiah was a favourite of the king, he was not the sort of man who would help Josiah's sons to grow up as their father had.

It was a grim outlook, but there were a few relatives of Josiah who were more like their king. One of these men was Zaccai. He and his wife Abigail had shown generosity and hospitality during Josiah's first Passover and they had

---

[12] Psalm 106:37-38; Numbers 35:33

continued to obey God's laws of worship. A little less than a year after that Passover, they had been blessed with the birth of a son whom they named Daniel.

Over the next few years, particularly after I became a priest and started to spend more time in Jerusalem, I was to see him grow and behold in him an example of what Josiah had achieved as a righteous king. Josiah had encouraged Zaccai and Abigail in their faith, and Daniel became a child of faith who later grew into a young man of faith and remarkable self-discipline. In many ways, he reminded me of Josiah, with his choice to serve God from an early age. He was also blessed with extraordinary ability.

It was in Daniel and a few others like him that the real success of Josiah was seen. If only he had been Josiah's son and become the next king!

☙

Not long after my father's death, I missed another wedding.

It was a wedding about which I had very mixed feelings. I was later told that the bride looked lovely, and I could well believe it – her face and her voice still troubled me when I let down my guard.

Yes, Shobai and Maacah married, and I was not surprised. My two short visits to Bethel over the previous two years had prepared me for the event, and I was pleased in a muddled sort of a way. They were both faithful worshippers of Yahweh and would help each other to maintain their faith; for that I could have rejoiced. Shobai had overcome his sadness at the death of Eglah, his first wife, and I was sure that Maacah would do her best to make the rest of his life happy. Surely her cooking would be enough to please anyone!

I was invited, and even urged, to attend the celebrations, but the command of God – still fresh and uncomfortable in my mind – forbade it:

> " 'You shall not go into the house of feasting
> to sit with them, to eat and drink.
> For thus says the Lord of hosts, the God of Israel:
> Behold, I will silence in this place,
> before your eyes and in your days,
> the voice of mirth and the voice of gladness,
> the voice of the bridegroom
> and the voice of the bride.' "[13]

God's words not only stopped me from going into the house of feasting with them, but also filled me with terror for them. These were my beloved friends, and Maacah could have been even more to me than that, except for other instructions God had given me:

> " 'You shall not take a wife,
> nor shall you have sons or daughters in this place.
> For thus says the Lord concerning the sons
> and daughters who are born in this place,
> and concerning the mothers who bore them
> and the fathers who fathered them in this land:
> They shall die of deadly diseases.
> They shall not be lamented, nor shall they be buried.
> They shall be as dung on the surface of the ground.
> They shall perish by the sword and by famine,
> and their dead bodies shall be food
> for the birds of the air
> and for the beasts of the earth.' "[14]

How could I rejoice in the face of such a threat of all-embracing disaster? Many times, I went through God's words in my head, trying to find a loophole – but there was none. "This place" *could* have referred only to Judah,

---

[13] Jeremiah 16:8-9
[14] Jeremiah 16:2-4

but "this land" and God's announcement of himself as the God of Israel? My friends would be joining a group of people for whom my God had announced devastating suffering: brides and bridegrooms, for whom joy would be silenced; mothers and fathers, whose children would join them in an unlamented, unburied death – food for bird and beast.

Woe seemed to be layered upon woe; disappointment upon disappointment; confusion upon confusion; constraint upon constraint. Frustration and bitterness filled my mind for some days, exacerbated by God's further limitation that I could not even pray for my people!

What could I do? I desperately wanted to share their joy. How could I obey the command to keep away? But God's word was still like a fire within me, so I sadly sent the message of my refusal to Shobai, trying to explain without seeming to decry God's word; to warn without terrifying. They understood; they married; they suffered.

At least they understood my need to obey God's commands better than many members of my family. That was some consolation.

Should I have tried harder to stop their marriage? I knew the disaster that was to spring upon us, ravaging, wreaking havoc; I knew the effects on husbands, wives and children. I knew. Were my warnings strident enough? Would they have listened anyway?

At times, there is an inconsolable loneliness in being a prophet. But there is also a closeness to the living, loving God that I would not be without for anything else in life.

It seems that we cannot have both. In his love, God makes sure that the suffering which comes from closeness to him is never too great to be borne. And the rewards of fellowship with him are beyond description. I cannot hope to describe the closeness, purity and happiness that fill me when the presence of God ushers me into an awareness of eternal righteousness, of a time when all of the degrading guile of sin will finally be cut out of humanity. Sadness and loneliness still remain now, but the hope is so profound and irresistible that I can bear the current suffering without despair.

It was at about this time that I reached a sudden understanding of why I had not been able to attend my brothers' weddings either. Although God had not told me at that time that I must not join in rejoicing or sorrow, he had still manoeuvred events so that I could not do so. What had seemed to me mere coincidence, now seemed to have the fingerprints of God upon it.

Knowing beforehand all the constraints that were to be placed upon me might well have been too much for me at that early stage of my apprenticeship as a prophet. True, the limits were essential to a full enactment of the prophecies of Yahweh, but for an ordinary young man such as I was, they were very severe.

☙

So the appearance of national worship was all a sham. Well, not quite all – there were still some whose worship of Yahweh was wholesome, genuine, thankful and joyful. As I have said, King Josiah, a handful of his family and close relatives, a small minority of the priests and Levites, and a painfully small number of the rest of the people – these were genuine. They were a people within a people. God had chosen his nation, but his nation had rejected him. Only a remnant was left for whom God was truly their god.

A righteous king; a godless nation. A beautiful temple; a worship of pretence. Promised destruction; confident boasts of longevity. We were a nation of contradictions; but Yahweh, the righteous judge, has always seen through the pretence.

The reality of the nation in those days is best shown by several facts that may seem unrelated.

Judah's princes were growing up, and not one of them shared his father's love of Yahweh.

The leading priests were all very rich men.

Many prophets spoke in many towns of Judah. Most were attracted to Jerusalem at some time or other. In almost every case, their words contradicted the words God spoke to me.

In the eighteenth year of his reign, Josiah had encouraged the people to renew the national covenant with Yahweh, and they had agreed. In an amazing response to their young king's enthusiasm, the people had learned all about God's covenant and the Book of the Law. But nothing seemed to be able to overwrite the idolatry that was written irrevocably in their hearts. At one stage, God told me:

> " 'The sin of Judah is written with a pen of iron;
> with a point of diamond it is engraved
> on the tablet of their heart,
> and on the horns of their altars,
> while their children remember their altars
> and their Asherim,
> beside every green tree and on the high hills,
> on the mountains in the open country.' "[15]

Even the children remembered and longed for the altars Josiah had destroyed. It seems ludicrous, since those very altars had been used for burning children alive – but they still longed for them.

Life changed a little after my father's death. My mother moved back to the family home in Anathoth, while Azariah and Hephzibah spent most of their time in the High Priest's house in Jerusalem. Whereas my father had

---

[15] Jeremiah 17:1-3

only used the house in a limited way, and it had always been available for other priests to use when there was a need for accommodation, Azariah and Hephzibah now made it their own. Even my mother did not seem to feel welcome, and I certainly didn't. Instead, when I was in Jerusalem I began to spend more time with others whom I knew there: Shallum and Huldah, Zaccai and Abigail, my father's two brothers, and my cousin Hanamel.

I also spent quite a lot of time in the temple, finding great pleasure in prayer, continuing my work of examining the vast array of scrolls we now had available, and also getting to know more of the priests and Levites – though this last was a mixed experience.

Just a few days after Shobai and Maacah were married, God spoke to me about covenants. It was an afternoon in mid-summer, and I was sitting in a side room of the temple where quite a few scrolls were stored. I was reading a scroll of the Book of the Law, one of the original batch of thirty created at the command of King Josiah. This scroll was one of four stored in the temple, in different rooms. The requirement to keep them in different rooms had come from King Josiah himself, with the intention of making sure that it could never again happen that the Book of the Law should be lost. He felt that no disaster, natural or man-made, should ever be allowed to separate Israel from the laws of our God. Permission was required to read any of these copies of the Book of the Law, but I had been given permanent permission by my father shortly after the copies were finished, so I often came to this room to read the scroll. Few others did, although most of the priests and Levites revered these copies of the Book of the Law almost to the extent of worshipping them.

Anyway, that special day on which Josiah had read the Book of the Law to the people had been on my mind all day, and I was remembering the atmosphere and events of that day as I read a passage near the start of the scroll, frequently hearing Josiah's voice in my head and picturing him on the platform reading God's word.

Then I came to a section which filled my mind with pictures of long ago instead:

> "And you came near and stood at the foot of the mountain, while the mountain burned with fire to the heart of heaven, wrapped in darkness, cloud, and gloom.
>
> "Then the Lord spoke to you out of the midst of the fire. You heard the sound of words, but saw no form; there was only a voice.
>
> "And he declared to you his covenant, which he commanded you to perform, that is, the Ten Commandments, and he wrote them on two tablets of stone.
>
> "And the Lord commanded me at that time to teach you statutes and rules, that you might do them in the land that you are going over to possess."[16]

I was picturing Mount Horeb burning with a fire that filled the sky above to an unimaginable height and the voice of God thundering across the plain, while all the people cowered and looked for somewhere to hide. The picture was coming vividly to life in my mind when suddenly a fire was lit inside me. As with the people of Moses' day, I saw no form, but the voice reverberated within me, and its power and purity terrified and exhilarated all at once:

> "Hear the words of this covenant, and speak
> to the men of Judah and the inhabitants of Jerusalem.
>
> "You shall say to them,
> Thus says the Lord, the God of Israel:

---

[16] Deuteronomy 4:11-14

Cursed be the man who does not hear the words
of this covenant that I commanded your fathers
when I brought them out of the land of Egypt,
from the iron furnace, saying,
Listen to my voice, and do all that I command you.
So shall you be my people, and I will be your God,
that I may confirm the oath that I swore to your fathers,
to give them a land flowing with milk and honey,
as at this day."[17]

"So be it, Yahweh," I replied. It sounded fair – even generous.

God continued speaking, telling me that I must announce his words throughout Jerusalem and all Judah. It was a command that I must obey, and the words I was being given to speak were words that demanded obedience from others too. Months of work stretched out before me again, and I felt that I could already hear the responses I would receive. Even my own response was no longer the joyous welcoming of the work of God that I had felt some seven years before. I knew that this would be hard work. Unpleasant too.

But God had more to say:

"A conspiracy exists among the men of Judah
and the inhabitants of Jerusalem.
They have turned back
to the iniquities of their forefathers,
who refused to hear my words.
They have gone after other gods to serve them.
The house of Israel and the house of Judah have
broken my covenant that I made with their fathers.
Therefore, thus says the Lord,
Behold, I am bringing disaster upon them
that they cannot escape.

---

[17] Jeremiah 11:2-5

Though they cry to me,
I will not listen to them."[18]

Clearly, Judah's pretence of worship did not deceive God, and he saw their revival of idol worship too. A conspiracy is something planned in secret and often only gradually hatched in public. The nation was turning away from God, abandoning the covenant they had so recently confirmed. But they weren't telling Josiah – oh no! He was to be placated, and deceived, by a sham of worship.

---

[18] Jeremiah 11:9-11

Chapter 4

A king is only a king

Repeated criticism of idols and images has been my most common task as a prophet. God has instructed me to condemn the worship of Baal, Chemosh, Asherah, Molech, Milcom, the so-called Queen of Heaven, Tammuz, Bel, Merodach, and Amon – each by name.

In Judah, Baal is the most popular of all the false gods, and every imaginable immorality, perversion and cruelty is practised in his name. Children are slaughtered, molested, sold and neglected, all in the name of worshipping this "Lord". Needless to say, I can't blame Baal for this tragedy, since he is entirely a figment of deluded imaginations anyway! No, all of this corrupt behaviour comes from within the minds of the worshippers, people who choose to ignore the living God and instead define their own worship of a fictitious deity. The worship reflects the hearts of the worshippers, and the heart of man is desperately wicked.[19]

---

[19] Jeremiah 17:9

Yahweh has told us exactly how he wants us to worship him – he does not leave those decisions up to us. Yahweh's rules enshrine obedience, humility, goodness, love, honesty, faithfulness, justice and kindness as the touchstones of life for his people. In the short term, though, he does not force these characteristics on people, so corrupt religions flourish, in spite of the many prophets that he sends to beg or demand reform and to present these characteristics to the people. Sadly, very few have ever listened enough to change.

But I haven't yet mentioned another important principle that God gave me to emphasise. It happened soon after that memorable Passover in the eighteenth year of King Josiah. The word of God in the Book of the Law and in our other scriptures highlighted the importance of the Sabbath for the health of the nation. When God spoke to me about this, it seemed as if it must be particularly important, because the message still offered hope. If the nation turned around and began to keep the Sabbath, God said, then all the threats of destruction would be revoked. Needless to say, this filled me with hope and optimism, despite all of God's previous messages. Possibly, I thought, the nation had turned the corner and its next step would be along the upward path to godliness.

I suppose that I probably need to explain what the Sabbath is, now that so few people ever keep it. When God created the world, he did so in six days and then rested on the seventh.[20] As he led Israel to the promised land, he gave us the Ten Commandments, and one of them demanded that we keep God's Sabbath, a day of rest in commemoration of this event. For people who were not priests, their common, everyday work was forbidden on the Sabbath. Farmers must not plough or reap, shepherds must not shear or sell their sheep, fishermen

---

[20] Genesis 2:1-3; Exodus 31:17

must not fish or mend their nets, merchants must not buy or sell, scribes must not prepare scrolls or write on them. Even soldiers must not march or practise on the Sabbath – all the ordinary work was forbidden for all professions. Likewise, the women were not to cook or clean or do any other work around the house.

Funnily enough though, for priests it was quite different: they must only do the work of their profession! Sacrifices must still be made – in fact, there were even special sacrifices for the Sabbath.[21] The lamp must still be kept burning in the temple, skin diseases must still be examined, and baby boys must still be circumcised on the eighth day after their birth.[22] All other work around the home was forbidden for priests, as it was for everyone in Judah, including any foreigners who chose to live in our cities.

But in all this I am speaking purely theoretically.

Maybe it was the fact that priests had to work on the Sabbath that made them less concerned about whether other people kept the Sabbath. Whatever the reason, the people of Judah did not keep the Sabbath. Furthermore, the priests of Judah did not even try to teach people that they should keep the Sabbath. This one of the Ten Commandments had completely lost its meaning. In my study of our scriptures I found the record of a man in the wilderness who was executed at God's command for collecting sticks on the Sabbath,[23] yet I saw people collecting sticks every Sabbath, and doing anything else they chose as well. When God instituted the Sabbath in the wilderness, he forbade even the preparation of food on the Sabbath,[24] but we priests thought we knew better. We concentrated on the aspects of worship that would

---

[21] Numbers 28:9-10
[22] John 7:22-23
[23] Numbers 15:32-36
[24] Exodus 16:23; 35:2-3

keep people happy and avoided conflict. This was my father's legacy.

Keeping the Sabbath was a constraint on people's behaviour which almost everyone considered too restrictive and believed would lead to confrontation. It was bad for business, reduced economic activity and made Judah a laughingstock among the surrounding nations. There simply wasn't the will to obey. Yet in this we dishonoured God. In one of the lists of the Ten Commandments, God explained why we should keep this day as special each week:

> "For in six days the Lord made heaven and earth, the sea, and all that is in them, and rested the seventh day. Therefore the Lord blessed the Sabbath day and made it holy."[25]

Each Sabbath day was to remind us of God's creation through the six days of hard work and that one day of rest. The countries that surrounded us were to see this acknowledgement of God as a creator and learn from what they saw. With all the blessings God had promised if we kept his commandments, the nations around us should always have been watching us, trying to see why we were so successful. Instead, we watched our neighbours and copied their failures.

God gave me a message that spoke of the gates of Jerusalem and told me to speak his words at every gate in the city,[26] so I visited each of the gates, one after another, and spoke God's word to any who would hear:

> " 'Thus says the Lord:
> Take care for the sake of your lives,
> and do not bear a burden on the Sabbath day
> or bring it in by the gates of Jerusalem.
> And do not carry a burden out of your houses

---

[25] Exodus 20:11
[26] Jeremiah 17:19

on the Sabbath or do any work,
but keep the Sabbath day holy,
as I commanded your fathers.
Yet they did not listen or incline their ear,
but stiffened their neck,
that they might not hear and receive instruction.

" 'But if you listen to me, declares the Lord,
and bring in no burden by the gates of this city
on the Sabbath day,
but keep the Sabbath day holy and do no work on it,
then there shall enter by the gates of this city
kings and princes who sit on the throne of David,
riding in chariots and on horses, they and their officials,
the men of Judah and the inhabitants of Jerusalem.
And this city shall be inhabited forever.' "[27]

But I think you can guess how many people really listened to Yahweh's words! Yes, King Josiah listened, but he didn't really need to. A few others listened also, but these were the few who already loved God's Sabbath. As a whole, the nation simply ignored both the message and its implied threat of destruction. And by ignoring it, they missed their opportunity of reconciliation with God.

A king is only a king. A king cannot control the thoughts or secret actions of his nation.

℞

615 BC – the 25th year of King Josiah

As I got to know them better in the later years of King Josiah's reign, I found that Zaccai and Abigail had a few relatives and friends who still held to the covenant they had made before God at the great gathering when King Josiah had read the Book of the Law to all of the people. Some of these developed a faith that they passed on to

---

[27] Jeremiah 17:21-25

their children, and some of those children later carried their faith to Babylon and showed their conquerors the power of the living God in whom they trusted.

But they were few in number.

One of Zaccai's younger relatives was a man named Zephaniah, the son of a second cousin of King Josiah.[28]

Zaccai had mentioned Zephaniah to me a few times, but it was not until the twenty-fifth year of Josiah that I actually met him for the first time. Apparently, he had asked to meet me, and Zaccai arranged the meeting and introduced us.

"Jeremiah, this is my young relative Zephaniah," said Zaccai with a smile. "I'm sure you will be pleased to meet him; he is very much your type of man – particularly now."

"The Lord be with you, Zephaniah," I said, looking closely at him and wondering what Zaccai meant. I saw a man who appeared a few years younger than myself, probably about twenty-five years old, with brown eyes, straight dark hair and a striking reddish beard. His rounded face had a look of pleasant openness, with a hint of tenacity and courage mixed in.

"The Lord bless you, Jeremiah," he replied, and his voice was light and smooth. He looked a little nervous, as if he knew what he wanted but felt a little unsure of himself.

---

[28] Zephaniah 1:1 tells us that Zephaniah was a fourth-generation descendant of a man called Hezekiah and that he prophesied in the time of King Josiah. Since people are rarely introduced by listing so many generations of ancestors, the most likely reason for doing so here is that it refers to King Hezekiah. Being one generation further from Hezekiah than Josiah, Zephaniah was probably younger than Josiah and Jeremiah. Hence, this story assumes that his prophesying began towards the end of Josiah's reign, in the twenty-fifth year.

I looked back to Zaccai and asked, "Zaccai, your introduction was a little obscure; what do you mean by 'your type of man'?"

"He is a man of God," said Zaccai simply, "and he has something to tell you."

Turning back to Zephaniah, I looked at him questioningly.

"God has spoken to me," responded Zephaniah eagerly. "He has given me words for Judah."

I was excited, but cautious. I knew of too many false prophets.

"How did it happen?" I asked Zephaniah, "and what was his message?"

"It was completely different from anything I have ever experienced before," he said, intently, leaning forward towards me as he spoke, before biting his lip and looking away as if trying to find the right words to describe his experience. I already knew from my discussions with Huldah that God does not communicate with all of his prophets in the same way, so I waited with interest.

"One night, just last week," he said, "I was praying to Yahweh when suddenly a light appeared in the room. I had been praising and thanking God for his love for and patience with our nation. Then with the light came a voice – a disembodied voice. It sounded like a man's voice in some ways, but it was also different. I had the feeling that I would still have been able to hear it however far away I moved, or even if I had covered my ears. Ever since, I have been trying to find a way to properly describe it."

"What did the voice say, Zephaniah?" I probed, wanting to check the message before concentrating too much on the method.

"Ah, well… it was a message of total destruction and devastation," he replied sadly, looking away and shaking his head. "He warned me how near it was, coming faster and faster, and described how it would affect Judah and all the surrounding nations." He turned back again. "It was horrible," he finished, speaking slowly and now looking intently at me. He seemed to be looking for encouragement and support – reassurance that the situation was not really so dire, that destruction would not arrive too soon.

But I felt suddenly cold inside, and fear gripped me as it had done when I had first received similar messages from Yahweh twelve years before. Could it be that I had become blasé about this repeated horrifying vision of a terrifying future? Had I ceased to deliver God's warnings with the power of terror that God wanted from me? Was Zephaniah being given the same message because he would tell the people with more authenticity?

All of a sudden, I wondered whether I had been failing God by allowing my expectation of an immediate fulfilment to become blurred or blunted. Had being a prophet become just a job to me instead of an urgent interruption to national life, a critical emergency?

These ideas sprang into my mind instantly, but a proper examination of them took several hours when I had some spare time, later. It woke me up.

"God told Huldah the prophetess that the disasters foretold in the Book of the Law would not happen in the time of Josiah," I countered.

"Ah, yes," he mused, "I had forgotten that. That makes me feel better."

"But should it?" I questioned, pondering whether this very confidence was one of the reasons why my own prophesying had lost some of its spark – and already I had no doubt that it had done.

"What do you mean?"

"I'm not suggesting that this will happen, but what if Josiah had a fatal accident today, or suddenly became very sick and died, and then we heard that an army was marching south through Israel? The disaster could come upon us within only a week or two!"

"But Josiah is perfectly healthy," Zephaniah objected.

"Yes, but God is in control. God has made it clear that his patience is exhausted, and I feel that he wants to begin the punishment immediately. Maybe in some way God is being limited by his love for Josiah." The thought was a little frightening, because Josiah had been my confidence for the past twelve years.

"But God also says that he gives long life to the righteous, and he has promised Josiah that he will die in peace, hasn't he?" argued Zaccai, who had been listening silently to our conversation.

"Yes, I don't think we need to worry about this for decades," agreed Zephaniah. "The king is only thirty-three years old, and a thirty-three-year-old can still expect to live for a long time, surely?"

I couldn't argue with them, but Zephaniah had stirred an uncertainty in me that left me feeling uncomfortable. I recall asking myself at the time how long Josiah was likely to live. Since I had no way of knowing, I resolved to do my best to go back to delivering God's messages with the urgency their words demanded, remembering that their worst horrors could conceivably be fulfilled within weeks if God chose that path.

For a while we three continued to discuss our hopes that the nation would be blessed with Josiah as its king for another thirty, forty or even fifty years. Then Zaccai left to carry out some work for King Josiah and Zephaniah and I were left alone. We turned our attention back to the words God had spoken to him and he took out a small scroll on which he had written the words of God so that he could remember them exactly.

"God's words spoke of a destruction like that of the flood," Zephaniah began as he unrolled the scroll and began to read. "He said:

" 'I will utterly sweep away everything
from the face of the earth,' declares the Lord.

" 'I will sweep away man and beast;
I will sweep away the birds of the heavens
and the fish of the sea,
and the rubble with the wicked.
I will cut off mankind
from the face of the earth,' declares the Lord."[29]

"If it hadn't been for the words that followed, I would have thought that this warning spoke of total destruction for everyone on earth," he said, frowning. "But then God seemed to make it clear that this referred particularly to Judah, and maybe the nations around her too – the Philistines, Moab and Ammon; even as far as the Assyrians."

"Was it a long message?" I asked. "Did you have any conversation with God?"

"Oh no," he answered quickly, looking a little shocked, "there was no discussion. I wouldn't dare speak to God!"

"I didn't have a choice," I said, drily. "He asked me questions. I had to answer."

"I still don't think I would be brave enough!" Zephaniah said, shivering.

"How long was he speaking to you for?" I asked, deciding not to point out that one does not refuse to answer Yahweh!

---

[29] Zephaniah 1:2-3

"Just a short time – I think." Zephaniah was looking thoughtful, and I felt that I understood. Time seems to be very flexible with Yahweh.

"Was the message all given at one time?" I pursued. "And do you think it is finished?"

"He spoke to me quite briefly on the first night, and then again on the next night. The third night he spoke for longer, and finished with a message of marvellous hope. I have not heard any more from him since then.[30] Will he speak to me again, do you think?"

"Three nights in a row! He has never spoken to me like that. I cannot tell whether he will speak to you again or not. We are all spoken to at his choice, not our own. He is Yahweh," I concluded, before asking, "Can I see what you have written?"

Zephaniah silently handed me the scroll, and I unrolled it. It did not take me long to read it, and there could be no doubt that the mind behind these words was the same mind that had initiated the words that still burned so brightly within me. It was an amazingly encouraging experience to have another prophet around, another person for whom God was alive and through whom God spoke. The feeling of loneliness that had characterised my time as a prophet was pushed back a little. It felt good.

As I read, I noted God's condemnation of priests and prophets, as well as a special comment about nobles and the king's sons:

> "I will punish the officials and the king's sons
> and all who array themselves in foreign attire."[31]

---

[30] The book of Zephaniah tells us nothing about how or when Zephaniah was given the prophecy that bears his name.
[31] Zephaniah 1:8

There was no doubt about it. Our nobles and the king's sons did mostly wear foreign clothes. And, of course, this meant that the blue cord that is at the corner of all our outer garments – intended to remind us of God's laws[32] – was always missing.

As a prophet, God had sent me to speak against my relatives, and now Zephaniah was in the same position. The king's sons were his relatives, just as the priests were mine. But God's words have been causing friction in families ever since the time of Cain and Abel, so we shouldn't be surprised when our experience is no different.

Several of Josiah's sons were young men by that time, and they were making it increasingly clear that once their father was no longer there, their choices would lead the nation towards the foreign ways and foreign gods that Yahweh had been condemning throughout our history as a nation. Josiah's sons loved them. And the oldest two, Eliakim and Jehoahaz, were the worst.

Whereas our family had always eaten together and I had known my father well, the king's sons lived quite a different life. Their father was almost a stranger to them, and I pondered whether there was any other way that it could have been. Josiah was a very busy man. His dedication to his nation and his position as king meant that he had no spare time, not even to allocate to his sons. Rather, it was their mothers and a few servants who had brought them up in most ways, and the nation was to pay a high price for this. When looked at in this way, the task of training the next king was actually one of the most important jobs in the kingdom – but most kings paid little attention to it. Maybe that is one of the reasons why so many of our kings have been so different from their fathers.

---

[32] Number s 15:38-39

Zephaniah's words from God were just as scathing as mine – and how that encouraged me! Eliakim and Jehoahaz were not exactly Zephaniah's close relatives, but he was being sent to censure their behaviour and that of the nobles of Judah. And it didn't stop there either:

> "Her officials within her are roaring lions;
> her judges are evening wolves
> that leave nothing till the morning.
> Her prophets are fickle, treacherous men;
> her priests profane what is holy;
> they do violence to the law.
> The Lord within her is righteous; he does no injustice;
> every morning he shows forth his justice;
> each dawn he does not fail;
> but the unjust knows no shame."[33]

Josiah's reign was a time of prosperity in some ways. To be sure, there were intermittent droughts,[34] but in general there was a greater stability and security. People were able to concentrate on their farming: ploughing, sowing, reaping and threshing. The poor, widows and orphans were able to be lifted out of poverty by the wise rule of King Josiah.[35] When everyone is better off, the poor are also, but Josiah also helped the poor directly by making sure that tithes and presents were distributed to the poor as they needed them. Widows and the fatherless were specifically assisted. Not only that, but when they were oppressed by the rich, they were given true justice that money could not pervert.

The rich were not pleased. The judges continued to cheat and take bribes where they could, but they had to be careful to avoid being noticed by the king, so they were cautious enough that most of the time what they

---

[33] Zephaniah 3:3-5
[34] Jeremiah 3:3
[35] Jeremiah 22:15

dispensed was quite close to justice. The priests corrupted God's laws and made the holy unclean, but I only learned that in detail after I was ordained as a priest.

There were also some beautiful and challenging words in Zephaniah's scroll:

> "Seek the Lord, all you humble of the land,
> who do his just commands;
> seek righteousness; seek humility;
> perhaps you may be hidden
> on the day of the anger of the Lord."[36]

Humility: something I had always struggled to learn, and found hard to unite with the immoveable stubbornness God had commanded me to have. Still, if Moses had been able to achieve it, I would have to just keep working.

◈

Confirmation from another prophet at that time was consoling. It is not easy when you know that the reigning monarch is striving for righteousness and yet all of God's messages condemn his nation. Audiences respond with hostility and anger. You see, when there is a righteous king, the nation seems to feel that it can bask in the reflected glory of his wisdom and godliness – even when they are doing all they can behind his back to undermine that godliness. They take any criticisms of the nation as personal reflections on the king. Human beings really do not seem to be very rational!

I did not meet Josiah very often during those years towards the end of his reign. He was busy with his work and I was busy with mine. At times, he sought me out to discuss the nation and its progress when measured against the word God had spoken. At times, I sought him out with

---

[36] Zephaniah 2:3

new messages from God. He was probably a little upset by my constant criticism of his nation, but he understood that these were not aimed at him personally, although they did reflect how well he was directing the nation into God's ways. But, after all, a king is only a king: he has some broad control, but he cannot exercise fine hour-by-hour control over the lives and thoughts of millions of people.

However, my prophesying in the time of Josiah was often met with aggressive criticism from others due to my perceived attacks on their beloved King Josiah, while many others responded aggressively because they heard criticism of themselves in the words God made me speak.

℘

614 BC – the 26th year of King Josiah

When God first appointed priests, he ordered that they should begin their work as priests at the same age as other Levites began their work: thirty years of age.[37]

Those of us who were descended from Aaron were trained from childhood to prepare us for our work as priests. But there was also a period of specific learning and preparation for all Levites that had originally begun at age twenty-five[38] though this had been lowered to twenty years old by David[39] in acknowledgement of the fact that the tabernacle no longer needed to be carried around. From that age, all male Levites began to learn what was required, and also to help with minor tasks around the temple. By the age of thirty, Levites and priests were considered ready to take on their inherited work in its entirety.

---

[37] Numbers 4:2-3
[38] Numbers 8:24
[39] 1 Chronicles 23:25-32

My training as a Levite and priest had been intermittent, and at times I had missed months of instruction. Being present in Jerusalem for the feasts had allowed me to learn and practise the duties of the descendants of Kohath and to observe the duties of priests. Learning the methods of identifying different diseases and assessing the value of different offerings required a lot of attention to detail and helped me to realise the importance of holiness and cleanliness to God. It also helped me to begin to understand the need to concentrate on obedience at every level: the sometimes fine detail of calculating tithes, as well as the wide vista of loving-kindness, faithfulness, justice and mercy that God has told us are so important to him.[40]

In the twenty-sixth year of Josiah, I turned thirty.

There was some opposition to my becoming a priest at all, and some suggested that I had abandoned my calling as a priest for that of a prophet. In the end, though, it was agreed that I should be ordained as a priest. I never knew what my brother Azariah's opinion on this question was: I never asked and he never volunteered the information.

As High Priest, I did speak to him about my limitations and divided responsibilities. In our discussions, I made it clear that I would continue to obey any commands from God to prophesy, but that I would do my very best to be clean in God's sight at all times.

From that time on, I saw the work of the temple from the inside. What I saw fitted with the words God had spoken through both Zephaniah and me: even in the days of Josiah, the priests served themselves, not God.[41]

---

[40] Exodus 34:6-7
[41] Jeremiah 8:10

Judah was my home and the areas of Israel were mostly occupied by my people, so messages to my people felt more important than messages to other nations.

Yet God did not feel that way. His original description of his work for me was as a prophet to the nations, and he continued to use me for that purpose. It was sometimes hard to step aside from my people and concentrate on the nations around.

At times, God wanted me to deliver messages to the nations directly, and then I travelled far and wide to obey him. But at other times, God delivered messages to other nations through their envoys or diplomatic representatives who came to visit King Josiah or his successors. In those days of international uncertainty, messengers were constantly being sent between nations, shoring up international cooperation or trying to form new alliances that would stand against the growing power of Babylon. Some of these representatives were men whom I had met in their own countries in earlier years, men climbing the ladder of diplomatic importance. Ahikam, the son of Shaphan, was always eager to meet these foreign representatives, and often we met them together. He taught me a lot about international relations through his questions and insightful comments. Some of these visitors tried to pump us for information with an eye to making friends among the influential men of Judah, but others were sincerely friendly and willing to listen patiently to the messages I had to convey.

These messages generally had a consistent theme: warnings of coming punishment and the threat from Babylon. Destruction was coming for all of these other nations.

But there were differences too. Some nations – including Edom – were warned of total destruction, permanent and complete, while the messages to others finished with a comforting reassurance that God would restore them in the future. The nations whose frightening warnings of coming suffering were tempered with this ray of future hope included Moab, Ammon and distant Elam.

When God gave me these messages, I spent many hours trying to understand the individual messages and the basis for his divine judgements. Why would Elam warrant restoration[42] while Edom deserved an overthrow like that of Sodom and Gomorrah?[43]

---

[42] Jeremiah 49:39
[43] Jeremiah 49:18

Chapter 5

Disaster

April, 609 BC – the 31st year of King Josiah

Late one afternoon, the watchmen at the Fish Gate saw an unusual cloud of dust approaching. They didn't want to overreact, but called their captain to pass on the news. As the portly captain ran heavily up from below, the cloud continued to approach until the watchers could distinguish a group of horsemen, riding hard. The breathless captain joined the watchmen, with his attendant at his heels. "What's going on?" he wheezed.

"Twelve horsemen, sir," answered the first watchman.

"Riding hard, sir," added the other.

"They look like they're ours," continued the first.

"But we're not sure, sir," cautioned the second.

"They sure are in a hurry, though," observed the first. "They'll be here very soon."

The captain mopped his brow and made a quick decision. Peace had characterised Josiah's long reign, but it was better to be safe than sorry.

He leaned over the edge of the wall towards the bustling throng in the gate below. "Guards!" he bellowed. "Guards! Call out the guards." He paused to take a breath, then bellowed again, "Take horses out to meet a party on the road. Hurry!"

Guards stationed at the gate acknowledged the orders and within seconds, two had mounted and were riding out through the gate as the crowds of ordinary citizens scattered out of their way. Two horsemen could not do much against twelve if the group's intentions were aggressive, but they could slow them down and help to determine their intent.

Another two were mounting to follow as the captain shouted once more, "Now shut the gates." He knew that it was probably unnecessary, but King Josiah was rather strict about that sort of thing. His guards and his army would never allow a sudden attack like that launched by the Assyrians against his grandfather Manasseh. Caution was better than careless confidence.

Under the arch and away galloped the second pair of riders and immediately the guards began to close the heavy wooden gates. Many of the merchants hawking their wares near the gate were quickly packing up their goods and several travellers hurried to slip through the rapidly shrinking gap into the safety of the city.

The gates closed with a thud, blocking the view of happenings outside the gate for all those below. The captain therefore decided to remain in his vantage point as the horsemen approached. However, there was one more thing he must do as the guards below lifted the cumbersome wooden bars into place as quickly as they could to hold the gates fast. "Go and tell our commander what is happening," he barked at his attendant, still a little short of breath. "Tell him, twelve horsemen approaching. Four sent out to intercept. Fish Gate closed. Awaiting developments."

By this time, the first pair of guards were approaching the twelve riders and the captain turned back to watch the encounter. The distance was still too great to see or hear exactly what was happening, but the guards seemed to welcome the galloping horsemen and quickly turned their horses to ride back to the city with them. The second pair did the same when they reached the group, and now sixteen riders were galloping the remaining short distance to the city walls where the gates remained closed firmly against them.

"Open up," shouted the first rider in a gravelly voice as he abruptly reined in his horse, directly beneath the excited watchmen and the portly captain. "We have news for the king!"

"What news?" called the captain, leaning over the parapet.

"Pharaoh Neco has invaded the land!" replied the dusty horseman. "We were guarding the frontier this morning when thousands of troops came marching up along the coast road. Pharaoh's army commanders told us to stand aside. They said they were not coming with any aggressive intent, but were just passing through on their way north." He held up a bag and added, "Pharaoh Neco has sent a message to King Josiah."

One of the guards the captain had sent out was deep in conversation with one of the dusty horsemen from the south, and it was clear that they knew each other. The captain was convinced. "Open the gates," he shouted, and the gates slowly opened. It was three days' hard march from the southern frontier, yet these horsemen had managed to arrive in Jerusalem before dark on the same day they had left the border. Their urgency had given King Josiah as much time as it was possible to give him. What happened next was up to the king.

While the guards returned to their duties, twelve sweating, dusty horses clattered through the gate into the city, their exhausted riders sweating profusely in the late afternoon warmth. Their work was done and soon they would be enjoying the rest and relaxation their hard riding had earned. Except for the leader, that is – he must first ensure that Pharaoh Neco's message reached the king.

☙

Josiah had reigned for 31 years. Another of our shared birthdays had passed at the end of the winter, and I was now 35 years old. Already, I had spent more than half of my life as a prophet to the nations.

The Assyrian empire was in its death throes. Almost three years before, Nineveh had been sacked by the victorious armies of Media and Babylon. However, its king had fought his way out of the city and retreated north to Haran[44] on the road between Nineveh and Carchemish. Just last year, Nabopolassar king of Babylon and Cyaxares king of Media had conquered Haran too, and the last king of Assyria had withdrawn again to marshal his forces and seek further support. Egypt had agreed to come to their aid, and it was on this errand that Pharaoh Neco was now marching urgently north.

I learnt many of the details of these events later on from Ahikam, the son of Shaphan, who was by that time one of King Josiah's closest confidants. We had met at intervals over the years because we moved in similar circles: he as a member of the nobility, and I as one of the High Priest's family. The position of High Priest was important, and riches have always guaranteed social importance. Ahikam's strong interest in international politics and diplomacy had also led him to approach me

---

[44] A way-point for Abraham on the way from Ur to Canaan (Genesis 11:31; 12:4). Also known as Harran.

whenever I returned from any visits to other nations – and anyway, we enjoyed each other's company. We also shared a love of Josiah our king. At the time when these events took place, I was in Syria, delivering yet another message of warning to yet another king who didn't want to hear it. Looking back now, it reminds me of the time when the Book of the Law was discovered and I was in Moab. Had I been there, I might have been able to offer some useful advice, but instead God made sure that I was a long way away offering his advance notice of trouble to unbelieving foreigners.

By the time that King Josiah had the opportunity to read the scroll from Pharaoh Neco, the Egyptian army was already marching north along the coast. The brief letter advised Josiah that Neco was simply passing through the land with no aggressive intent. He would, he wrote, be crossing the northern border into Syria as soon as possible, hurrying to meet those with whom he was at war.

There was little time to decide what to do – if indeed anything should be done at all.

Before darkness fell, the entire city was agog with speculations which led people in all directions at once. Fearful souls were concerned that it was all a trick and that Egypt was really invading Judah.

Others felt that Pharaoh Neco could be believed and should be left alone to look after his own business. "Let well enough alone," they murmured sagely, "and don't go looking for trouble."

Some said that it was utter cheek and a gross impertinence; Pharaoh should be shown that Judah's good will could not be presumed upon or taken for granted in this way!

Most of King Josiah's advisors seem to have taken this last attitude – or maybe it was simply that the king himself felt this way. Whatever the source of the contagion, this feeling carried the day, and within hours of the news arriving, mounted couriers had been dispatched to order most of the standing army to meet the king in the north of Israel near Jezreel. Amazingly, several messengers from units of the army in areas south of Jerusalem arrived in the city on horseback with the dawn to confirm the marching arrangements and assure Josiah of their support in the crisis.

Already, Pharaoh Neco would be just three days' march from the valley of Jezreel, and within another two days after that he would have crossed the northern border into Syria. It was felt that he must not be allowed to reach there without some decisive military action on the part of Josiah's army. The resulting urgency drove everybody to desperate action, and little time was spent in reflection.

Ahikam told me that Josiah had left the city before midday, marching out with his advisors and a few units from Jerusalem.

Though additional troops joined the column as the king made his way north through the hill country, it was still a relatively small army that arrived at the head of the valley of Jezreel on the third day after a hurried but exhilarating march.

Scouts had kept the king informed about the progress of the Egyptian army, and it was known that the fast-moving army of Judah was now ahead of Neco's larger, more ponderous army. Small groups of reinforcements continued to arrive with every passing hour, and later in the day, the army moved cautiously down the valley, keeping close to the south bank of the river Kishon. Everything depended on being within reach of Neco and his men as they marched through the pass at Megiddo.

Spirits were high despite the weariness of all who followed Josiah. Surely a good night's sleep would cure the problem of tiredness, they thought, and everyone agreed that Yahweh would help them in the next day's battle. Scouts were dispatched to check on conditions further down the valley and to warn the local farmers that their flourishing fields would probably be the scene of a battle on the next day.

A feeling of confidence – even cockiness – filled the army, despite, or perhaps because of, its lack of experience. No major battles had been fought in Judah during the reign of King Josiah – had not God promised that he would live and die in peace?

Towards evening, four envoys on four beautifully adorned chargers trotted into the camp beside the river bringing King Josiah a message from Pharaoh Neco.

The envoys were dressed in typically scanty Egyptian clothing, but despite this, it was clear that no expense had been spared on their costumes and ornamentation. Their minimal attire stood in marked contrast to the fulsome clothing of the Israelite guards who surrounded them immediately on their arrival. Though Josiah's army had been congratulating themselves on their speedy but stealthy positioning in the strategic valley of Jezreel, Pharaoh's scouts had obviously not been idle, and Neco was clearly far from ignorant of their presence and identity.

The four men dismounted and explained their mission. Clearly they were important men and King Josiah's guards treated them with great respect as they led them to the king. Their leader wasted no time in delivering a message that was both simple and blunt: "Pharaoh Neco says, 'What have we to do with each other, king of Judah? I am not coming against you this day, but against the house with which I am at war. And God has commanded me to hurry. Cease opposing God, who is with me, lest he destroy you.' "[45]

---

[45] 2 Chronicles 35:21

Beyond acknowledging the envoys courteously, King Josiah did not respond to the message in any way. He offered the envoys food and drink and invited them to share his hospitality, but they were in a hurry to be gone. As they remounted and rode away, King Josiah and his advisors withdrew to his tent for consultation. The discussion went back and forth and the situation was argued from all possible angles. Finally, the king made his decision: he would face Neco in battle whatever the consequences – Pharaoh Neco must be lying about the command from God.

CR

Early the next morning, Josiah gave the command and his small army marched further down the valley of Jezreel towards Megiddo. Perched as it was on a hill beside the main road where it led out of the pass and down into the Valley of Jezreel, Megiddo was ideally placed to watch the Valley of Jezreel and guard the pass.

Stopping quite some distance short of the road, the army posted watchmen and waited for the arrival of the Egyptian army.

Josiah's scouts had reported that the Egyptian army had chosen to cross from the coastal plain into the Valley of Jezreel through this particular pass and would pass the walls of Megiddo at about noon. And so it proved. Not long after taking their positions, the watchmen and soldiers of Judah looking up towards the pass beside Megiddo saw scattered groups of men begin to appear suddenly on the skyline. Gradually, the skyline filled with men, and the dust from thousands of tramping feet rose on the still air. Chariots moved on the flanks of the army, and the number of men visible continued to increase.

Slowly the army seemed to flow down the hill towards the valley. Wave after wave of infantry passed the city standing off to one side of the pass with its gates firmly closed.

For the small army of Judah, this was a frightening revelation of a foe of overwhelming size. Outnumbered by infantry, outnumbered by archers and outnumbered by chariots, their only hope could be faith in Yahweh.

And this faith would prove to be misplaced – or rather, misdirected.

Josiah waited, and the commanders of the army waited also. Their plan of engagement had been developed in discussions the night before: Josiah would pretend to be just an ordinary charioteer. The commanders would take the foremost positions in the main body of the infantry while Josiah's chariot moved in obscurity on the southern flank, so that Neco's men had no specific target to aim for. Despite being outnumbered, the army must fight with confidence and faith, relying on God to give them the victory.

Pharaoh's army reached the plain and split into two parts. The majority of the army followed the main road north, completely ignoring the army of Judah. The remainder of the army swung towards Josiah and his waiting men, still outnumbering them, but on a less formidable scale.

At the head of this horde was Pharaoh Neco, riding easily in his light but colourful chariot, surrounded closely by his bodyguard and flanked on either side by battle commanders and trumpeters. Chariots trotted along the southern fringe of the host, forming a widening pincer movement as they advanced and slowly separated from the main body of infantry. Disciplined and steady, measured and patient, the armies seemed almost calm as they drew closer together. Quietly, Josiah's army stood their ground as the cream of Pharaoh's army advanced slowly towards them.

Suddenly, signals came from the Egyptian centre and the tempo increased. Horses were urged to a gallop and the chariots on the southern edge began to pull further ahead of the infantry. Egyptian soldiers broke into a run and the time for battle drew near.

Galloping hooves, shouting men, blaring trumpets: but still the men of Judah waited in silence. It was not until the Egyptian chariots on the southern flank passed a chosen point that the trumpeters within Judah's centre suddenly blew the alarm. Shouts came from every throat, soldiers ran forward and the chariots of Judah threw themselves at the foe.

The distance had been chosen carefully. Judah's archers were able to draw and loose immediately, and the Egyptians were caught off guard. For a brief instant, Judah held the advantage, but the real business of battle had barely begun.

Neco's strategy was shown at once by his chariots, which repeatedly made lightning dashes towards the infantry, feinting and withdrawing as they looked for the one target they sought. Josiah was that target, and Pharaoh Neco seemed to have instructed his forces to specifically search him out and destroy him. Persistently Neco's racing chariots approached the footmen, spearmen, archers and chariots of Judah, delivering volleys of arrows before quickly retreating as they failed to identify their prey. Two of the four envoys of the previous evening were in the leading chariots as they repeatedly approached and withdrew.

Battle had now been joined between the infantry columns, and the fierce hand-to-hand combat prevented the archers on either side from shooting near the battle line for fear of striking their own men.

It was at this point that Josiah, disguised, but riding in his own chariot on the southern flank, decided to move in towards the centre of the fighting. As he did so, other chariots followed him, some of which did their best to pass him to offer their king some protection against the enemy. They sped towards the unsuspecting foot soldiers, preoccupied as they were with bitter man-on-man fighting, and Josiah waved his arms and shouted, absorbed in the battle. Still more chariots followed, and soon a wedge of Judah's chariots was cutting a swathe through the Egyptian front lines and moving towards the centre. Some way back from the front line, Josiah perceived Pharaoh Neco in his chariot and altered course to ride directly towards him. Another shout broke from his lips, and in that instant, one of the envoys who had met Josiah the previous evening saw him and recognised him. He must have been an important man, because his chariot was right next to Neco's. His shout to Neco was drowned out by the tumult of battle, but he was near enough to reach out and grasp Neco's arm. He pointed at Josiah and shouted still louder, "There is Josiah, the king of Judah!"

Pharaoh Neco gazed at Josiah as he was fighting his way through the infantry, and signalled calmly to the archers in his bodyguard. They rallied to him, and with the help of his envoy, he showed them their target.[46]

Josiah was still valiantly fighting his way towards Neco using his sword and a short spear when the first arrow struck him in the chest. He knew at once that he was severely wounded, and immediately grabbed his chariot driver by the arm and cried, "Take me away, for I am badly wounded."[47] The driver did his best to turn around as quickly as possible, but as they slowed, Neco's archers had an easy target and many other arrows followed, striking Josiah again and again.

---

[46] 2 Kings 23:29
[47] 2 Chronicles 35:23

By the time the driver managed to turn the horses and guide them out of the fray, Josiah had slumped to the floor of the chariot and was gasping for breath.

As the chariot struggled back to the reserves where help might be found for the stricken king, a ragged shout went up from the Egyptians. The news was spreading. Josiah was badly wounded, they heard. Judah's soldiers faltered, and in that moment, the battle was lost. As an overflowing stream spreads out and covers everything in its path, so the army of Egypt spread over the field of battle and all fled before them.

Josiah, meanwhile, had been helped into his second chariot with its fresh horses and gasped out his instructions: "Take me away." His servants did their best to make him comfortable, but he was failing fast. The medical helpers had little hope, but they suggested taking the king to Jerusalem as quickly as possible. The chariot driver started the horses with the whip.

The battle was lost and their king badly wounded. Judah's army fled until they reached the hills where the chariots could pursue them no longer. In reality, Pharaoh Neco's victorious army did not pursue for long – it seemed that they really were in a hurry. Soon the reformed column was marching back to the road, hurrying north to rejoin their fellows. A few would stay to help the wounded, bury the dead and strip the fallen soldiers of Judah, but the bulk of the successful troops would be reunited with the rest of the army before nightfall. This small delay would not matter too much, but when Pharaoh Neco returned, he would make Judah pay. Handsomely.

Bouncing roughly in his chariot, Josiah was close to death as the chariot passed out of the valley of Jezreel, and well before the small convoy stopped for the night, the last great king of Judah was dead.[48]

This king had dedicated his entire life to the service of his God and his nation – from early childhood when most children were playing, carefree, with toys. Josiah had worked tirelessly and selflessly, right up until the day of his untimely death. Now his lifeblood had stained the green grass of Megiddo's valley, and painted a crimson trail on the road towards Jerusalem.

Josiah was dead, and what would become of Judah? The nation had fled before its enemies, and who would lead them now?

In ones and twos and in straggling groups of dispirited men, the defeated army of Judah made its way slowly south. No-one knew what had happened to their king, or whether he was dead or alive – but they had their fears.

℈

Some men, however, hurried back to Jerusalem. For them, the future beckoned, and a delay could lose them much. Josiah's senior advisors were hard on the heels of the chariot that carried the body of their king, and entered the city while the news was still spreading.

Eliakim, Josiah's oldest son, had been with the army near Megiddo, but his position had been with the reserves.[49] He was not popular with the leaders of the army and he knew it. He was equally unpopular with the people of Judah, and he knew that too, but he didn't care.

---

[48] Combining 2 Kings 23:30 and 2 Chronicles 35:24

[49] We are not told whether or not Eliakim was present at the battle when Josiah was killed. However, a slow return from the battle on his part might explain how the people of the land were able to appoint his younger brother as king.

The kingship was his by birthright, but until the crown actually sat upon his head… well, it was best to return to Jerusalem as soon as possible.

Nevertheless, indolence inevitably delayed his journey. Each night, Eliakim interrupted his journey early, settling down for an indulgent meal, served by his attendants, and a comfortable night's rest. Each morning, he set off correspondingly late, with the result that an extra day had been added to the journey before the walls of Jerusalem came in sight.

As his chariot entered through the Benjamin Gate, Eliakim heard cheers from the direction of the temple. Swiftly, he climbed down from his chariot and made his way to the gate of the temple.

As he entered the gate, he saw crowds of people thronging the temple courts and was just in time to hear the shouts: "Long live King Jehoahaz!"

He was dumbfounded. The kingship was his! How could Jehoahaz, his younger brother, be there, standing before Azariah the High Priest and the cheering crowd, wearing a crown while anointing oil still dripped from his beard? There must be some mistake, he thought, and he strode arrogantly towards the front of the crowd to set it right. But as he approached the newly crowned king, the guards who separated the crowds from King Jehoahaz moved unobtrusively together to form a solid wall between Eliakim and his brother. The soldiers had their orders, and although none of them wanted to antagonise Prince Eliakim, the new king must be given complete protection.

Three of Josiah's advisors stepped forward and spoke quietly to Eliakim for a short while. As could be expected, though, his confusion quickly turned to an anger that began to attract attention, so the nobles led him off towards one of the temple buildings where the walls of an inner room would offer some privacy. These men had taken on a difficult task: trying to placate an impatient and self-important young man. However, while Eliakim was never happy with the appointment of Jehoahaz as king, these wise men somehow convinced him that being a prince had certain advantages over the demanding responsibilities of kingship.

Chapter 6

Looking back, moving forward

Josiah had been dead for two weeks by the time I returned to Jerusalem. News of the disaster had reached me in Syria within days of the catastrophic battle near Megiddo. Despite my initial disbelief, the details I heard had finally convinced me that Josiah really was dead. As quickly as I could, I delivered the message from God that had taken me to Syria, and a week later was making my urgent way home.

On arriving in Jerusalem, I searched out all the news I could find, and slowly pieced it all together.

By then, Jehoahaz was firmly established in the palace, having been appointed by the populace as soon as Josiah was known to be dead.[50] Although not a righteous or particularly endearing young man, Jehoahaz was better than Eliakim. Eliakim was violent, self-indulgent, self-satisfied, and greedy. The kingdom was better off without

---

[50] 2 Kings 23:30; 2 Chronicles 36:1

him, and I remember the relief I felt when I heard that he had not been made king.

King Josiah had been buried on the day his body had arrived in Jerusalem, but the great outpouring of grief from across the nation was still continuing.

No words could express my utter sorrow and desolation at the death of Josiah. He was a king without equal in some ways. No king before him had ever turned to God with such a singleness of purpose or dedication as King Josiah had.[51] From two generations of rulers who exemplified an evil so imaginative that it had outdone even the surrounding nations, had come a young child with a pious nature and godly desires. His unfeigned acknowledgement of his need for forgiveness was without equal in the annals of the kings of Judah and Israel. By all reports, his great-grandfather, Hezekiah, had been an amazing ruler, but Josiah had outshone even him in some ways.[52]

Humility was his trademark and had earned him the promise through Huldah that he would die in peace before the promised disaster from the north overtook the nation of Judah. Yet his death at the hands of Pharaoh's archers had been anything but peaceful.

What had gone wrong?

℘

Changes came quickly. The mourning over the death of Josiah seemed universal, but it was very hard to believe that it was completely genuine when the changes to society began immediately. Can someone really be genuinely sorry that their king is dead when they begin to do things he had forbidden before he is even in his grave?

---

[51] 2 Kings 23:25
[52] Compare 2 Kings 18:5 and 2 Kings 23:25.

I was not there, but I was told by friends who were there that some of the mourners brought small idols with them when they came to witness King Josiah being buried with his fathers.

By the time I returned, it was nearly two weeks since Jehoahaz had been anointed king, and idols and altars were already springing up again in many of the smaller streets of Jerusalem. The initial moves towards idol worship were surreptitious, since no-one could be quite sure of what the new king would do, but the quiet determination of evil was staking out its claim over the city.

For those of us who genuinely loved King Josiah, this was a time of deep sadness that had taken us all by surprise. Josiah was only 39 years old.

Even before arriving home in Anathoth, I had begun to write a lament about Josiah. His greatness amongst the kings of Judah is hard to overstate. Before him there was no king like him, who turned to the Lord with all his heart and with all his soul and with all his might, according to all the Law of Moses.[53]

After communing with others in Jerusalem who felt as devastated by the death of the king as I did, I completed this lament:

> My joy is gone; grief is upon me;
> my heart is sick within me.
> Behold, the cry of the daughter of my people
> from the length and breadth of the land:
> "Is the Lord not in Zion? Is her King not in her?
> The harvest is past, the summer is ended,
> and we are not saved."
> For the wound of the daughter of my people
> is my heart wounded;
> I mourn, and dismay has taken hold on me,

---

[53] 2 Kings 23:25

Josiah, your king, lies slain, and the enemy has prevailed.
When a king rules in justice and righteousness,
and the cause of the needy is his;
when a ruler will judge for the poor,
and precious are their ways in his sight;
then a people is blessed by the Lord
and he guards them in all of their ways.
Should not a king rule as David,
doing right in the eyes of the Lord?
Yet Josiah, your king, lies slain,
the glory of Judah is slain.
For these things I weep; my eyes overflow with tears,
for a comforter is far from me, one to revive my spirit;
my people are desolate, for the enemy has prevailed.
The servant of Yahweh has fallen in battle.
Alas, the great day of the Lord is near,
near and hastening fast;
for Josiah, your king, lies slain,
the glory of Judah is past.[54]

I was not the only one who wrote a lament for Josiah, and some of the other laments seemed much better written than mine, but one thing stood out: for anyone who loved Yahweh our God, the death of King Josiah seemed to be a terrible loss.

And so it proved. It was shown even in the brief reign of Jehoahaz, and it has been shown in the reign of each king since. As I write this diary and mull over the tragic events that have followed in Judah, I see ever more clearly just how quickly good can be snuffed out when its defenders are taken away.

Leaders cannot single-handedly change their people's hearts towards goodness, but they can act as a bulwark

---

[54] 2 Chronicles 35:25 tells us that Jeremiah uttered a lament for Josiah, but we are not told what he said. These words are selections from Jeremiah 8:18-21, 22:15-16, Lamentations 1:16, Zephaniah 1:14 and other places.

against wrong and force it to withdraw from public life. Allowing evil to take over in public life plants that evil so deeply in the heart of a nation that it can never be eradicated without some catastrophe taking place. Reformation can temporarily remove the visible weeds, but the roots are so deep that only total disaster can remove them.

King Josiah's death was like the start of a new spring for the roots of evil that had waited patiently in the heart of Judah. A vigorous growth of wickedness began immediately, and it was a growth that was stopped only by the flames and fury of Nebuchadnezzar's armies.

☙

One of the questions that continued to trouble my mind was, "Why did Josiah die?"

Had he not been promised a peaceful death?[55] — yet his death had been the direct result of war.

I mulled over this for many hours over several weeks: at first desperately trying to imagine how these events could fit in with God's promise, then wanting to be sure that I understood. Although I am still not certain that my final understanding is correct, I think it is. I do not include this section to condemn King Josiah. His righteous reign showed amazing strength, faith and obedience, and I would never want to take anything away from that. But in this case I had to resolve a conflict: how could God promise Josiah a peaceful death and then allow him to die in battle? How could I explain events and what could I learn from them?

These are my sad conclusions.

Sometimes God leaves us to work out problems for ourselves. When Josiah received the news that Pharaoh

---

[55] 2 Kings 22:20; 2 Chronicles 34:28

Neco's army had crossed into Judah, there was little time to make a decision as to whether anything was to be done before the army passed beyond Judah.

Little time, yes, but still time enough to ask God. After the discovery of the Book of the Law in the eighteenth year of his reign, Josiah had immediately sent to Huldah the prophetess to seek advice, and God had given it.

On this occasion, though, there were no enquiries. Whether it was the pressure of time – the need for a quick decision – or something else, Josiah did not consult any of the prophets he knew he could trust.

God had promised Josiah that he would die in peace, and no battles had arisen during his reign, from the time of that promise until the fateful day when the news about Pharaoh Neco arrived. Maybe that promise should have given Josiah the confidence that he could believe Neco, or at least ignore him if he couldn't quite believe him.

God's promises are always conditional on obedience, and I have concluded that Josiah should not have gone to fight Pharaoh Neco. My belief is that God really had sent Neco to fight alongside the declining Assyrian army against the armies who were taking over Assyria. Josiah should have left him alone.

If Josiah had avoided anything that was not peaceful because he was relying on God's promise of a peaceful death, events would have been different, and the peace with which God had blessed him throughout his reign would have continued until the very end – whenever that might have come.

Sadly, all of us fail, and I think this was a case where King Josiah lost his way and missed the path God would have wanted him to choose. How lucky we are to have a God who shows lovingkindness to the righteous even when we fail.

The end came so suddenly.

Many died in the Valley of Jezreel on that tragic day, but Josiah was the one whom the nation would miss most. None of his sons could replace him as a righteous king, and none had any intention of even trying.

CR

Most kings choose new advisors when they take over from their father, and Jehoahaz was no exception.

Those who advised King Josiah had had to be eager, or at least willing, to accept his insistence that Yahweh must be at the centre of a king's efforts to rule his kingdom.

Jehoahaz did not want advisors like that.

During his reign, God did not speak to me at all.[56] It was almost as if he did not exist. Maybe that was just a reflection of how short his reign would be.

Jehoahaz, or Shallum as he was sometimes known, led Judah for only three months, and it was a time of impending doom.

Pharaoh Neco had defeated Judah on his way north. When he returned from the north – whether he won or lost his battle with the armies of Babylon and Media – Judah could expect a time of retribution.

King Josiah's former advisors understood this, and would have explained it to King Jehoahaz – if he had been willing to listen.

But Jehoahaz chose new advisors and would not listen to the old ones. He refused to believe that Pharaoh Neco

---

[56] No chapters in Jeremiah make any reference to a time during the reign of Jehoahaz, and the sole mention of him is after he has been taken away. Jeremiah 1:3 lists the reigns during which Jeremiah heard from God, and does not include any reference to the time of Jehoahaz.

would return and that preparations should be made to defend Jerusalem.

As it happened, though, Neco didn't even wait until he could return to Jerusalem. After the battle of Megiddo, he marched north and his army set up a base at Riblah in the land of Hamath, to the north of Damascus. From there he sent to enquire about the state of the kingdom of Judah, and was advised that Jehoahaz had been appointed king and was reigning in Jerusalem.[57]

On receiving this information, Neco sent again to demand acknowledgement of his sovereignty over Judah, requiring Jehoahaz to go to meet him in Riblah. After a short period of consideration, King Jehoahaz departed for Riblah with his attendants and some of the advisors who had given him such false confidence.

He made the long journey north[58] confidently, but was welcomed with chains – and in chains he stayed while Neco concluded his successful campaign against Media and Babylon. Then a victorious Neco and his army returned south, going directly to Jerusalem.

Jerusalem was completely unprepared to defend herself, and Neco entered the city as a conqueror. No-one believed that they could beat him anyway – had not even Josiah fallen before him? And now it was reported that he had defeated the combined armies of Media and Babylon. Jehoahaz, their king, was displayed in chains before a cowed populace, and Neco announced that he could no longer be king. He had reigned for just three months.

---

[57] According to 2 Kings 23:33, Neco put Jehoahaz in chains in Riblah, while 2 Chronicles 36:3 says he deposed him in Jerusalem. There is no mention of any siege of Jerusalem or any other town. In the time of Zedekiah, Jerusalem withstood a siege for 18 months, so it appears that Jehoahaz attempted no defence. The description here endeavours to put together the details recorded.

[58] Riblah is about 350–400 kilometres (220–250 miles) from Jerusalem.

As the wise had predicted, Neco also came with a demand for tribute: 100 talents of silver and a talent of gold.[59] Yet again, the Egyptian Pharaoh had done his homework and knew the details of the royal family of Judah. He went into the palace, seated himself on the grand throne of Solomon and called in Eliakim, Josiah's oldest son. In a brief interview, he set out his requirements: Eliakim would be made king over Judah, and his first task was to arrange for the collection and payment of the tribute money. If he succeeded, he could remain king.

During the brief reign and subsequent enforced absence of his brother Jehoahaz, Eliakim had played the life of an idle prince, competing in some way with his brother. He had used imported timber from Lebanon in the decoration of his house, and a bevy of carpenters had been working on it even as Pharaoh Neco entered the city. Eliakim obviously decided that collecting the tribute money would be worth the effort, particularly since he would not be paying it – instead, Judah's nobles and the general populace would provide the money. Eliakim's advisors helped him determine the necessary rate of tax.

Eliakim was anointed king in the temple of Yahweh at Neco's behest. My brother Azariah, now thoroughly at home in the position of High Priest, led the ceremony with great solemnity, and Eliakim was publicly acknowledged as the new king of Judah – whether the people wanted him as their king or not. They didn't.

Pharaoh Neco then announced that the tribute must be collected immediately. He would not, he said, leave until the money had been delivered. Maybe he had heard what Eliakim was like, or maybe he was just naturally suspicious, but either way, his decision was wise. Had he

---

[59] 3.45 tonnes of silver (3.8 tons or 122,000 ounces) and 34.5 kilograms (75 pounds or 1,220 ounces) of gold.

left without the money, Eliakim would have done all he could to avoid payment. Some people can be trusted, but Eliakim was not such a man. Pharaoh's army remained encamped around Jerusalem, living off the fat of the land, and Eliakim was compelled to act quickly.

In the end, Eliakim did rather well out of it all: he took the money that he owed the workmen for redecorating his house and paid it all to Neco instead, as his contribution to the tribute.[60] Of course, the workmen still had to pay their own taxes in addition to the involuntary contribution they had already made through their king's "generosity".

Eliakim delivered the collected tribute to Neco and Pharaoh prepared to leave. In a parting interview with the new king, Neco announced a masterful test of loyalty: he changed Eliakim's name. From then on, Neco said, Eliakim was to be called "Jehoiakim". If Pharaoh Neco ever heard that he was using any other name, he would take it as an act of direct rebellion and respond accordingly.

Pharaoh Neco left Jerusalem and returned to Egypt, taking the deposed king with him. Jehoahaz was never to return to his native land.[61] God had rejected him.

---

[60] There is no record of this in the Bible. It is merely used as a picture of the behaviour of Eliakim that is described in Jeremiah 22:13-14.
[61] Jeremiah 22:11-12

Chapter 7

A new direction

September, 609 BC – the 1st year of King Jehoiakim

Pharaoh Neco had been gone only a week when God spoke to me again. I was staying in our home at Anathoth in which my mother now lived as a widow, and was in the scroll room, my favourite room in the house. I had spent many hours there over the years of Josiah's reign with a flickering lamp for company, reading huge numbers of scrolls, trying to sort out the wheat from the chaff. There were scrolls of the history of the world, scrolls of the original words of ancient prophets, and scrolls recording the collected wisdom of kings and masters of philosophy. There were scrolls in many different shapes and sizes, including some small sheets and even some torn fragments. I had devoured them all in many a late-night voyage through history and prophecy.

I had been savouring a Psalm of David describing the joy of worshipping in Jerusalem and the confidence that comes when kings judge in righteousness,[62] when I felt the familiar fire tingling in my bones and spreading slowly over my whole body. The Psalm urged me to pray for the peace of Jerusalem, and I was doing so when the fire of God engulfed me. Yahweh often seems to speak to me at times when I am already listening to his words or the words of his prophets. This time, it was the message I had been dreading.

My memories of Eliakim – or Jehoiakim as I must now call him – were not positive. What I knew of him through my own experience and the reports of others showed him to be a violent and godless man.

And Yahweh wanted me to pass on a message to him:

"Thus says the Lord:
'Go down to the house of the king of Judah
and speak there this word, and say,
"Hear the word of the Lord, O king of Judah,
who sits on the throne of David,
you, and your servants,
and your people who enter these gates.
Thus says the Lord:
Do justice and righteousness,
and deliver from the hand of the oppressor
him who has been robbed.
And do no wrong or violence to the resident alien,
the fatherless, and the widow,
nor shed innocent blood in this place.
For if you will indeed obey this word,
then there shall enter the gates of this house
kings who sit on the throne of David,
riding in chariots and on horses,
they and their servants and their people.
But if you will not obey these words,

---

[62] Psalm 122

> I swear by myself, declares the Lord,
> that this house shall become a desolation." ' "[63]

There were other words as well, all delivered at a steady pace, measured and methodical, as God described what he required of a king. Yahweh is amazingly patient, and he gives people many opportunities to repent – even when a man's past life gives little hope of redemption.

Would Jehoiakim welcome my words?

For the first time, I would have to speak to a king of Judah who would be unlikely to listen sympathetically to my message. It was a frightening thought.

Nevertheless, God's command must be obeyed, and I reflected on his promise of protection – offered as long as I stood resolutely on his side. That promise had always held true, although I still remembered that long-ago incident in the Valley of the Son of Hinnom[64] with some misgivings. However, I had concluded that the minor cuts and bruises I had suffered were not too bad – although they had been a surprise at the time.

In my experience, prophesying in Judah had always felt more dangerous than being a prophet to the nations. Foreigners always welcomed me patiently and even kings listened carefully as I conveyed the word of Yahweh to them, but when speaking to the people of Judah there were always undercurrents of anger, and barely controlled violence seemed to bubble near the surface. Thus far, though, Josiah's powerful presence had kept things under control – mostly.

My sleep was a little disturbed that night. I was feeling some of the same nervousness that I had felt when God had first shown me my life's work. It was like a new

---

[63] Jeremiah 22:1-5
[64] See Volume 1 – Early Days, Chapter 12.

beginning, after eighteen years of prophesying in the comfortable shadow of King Josiah.

Throughout those years, I had kept to my habit of early morning prayer, and that midsummer morning presented me with a stunning array of graduated hues, from the sable of night to the golden glint of day, as the edges of the sparse clouds were drawn in intricate detail with needle-sharp pens of sunlight. As I prayed, courage slowly returned to me under the calming hand of the master artificer.

As we ate our morning meal, I told my mother what I would be doing that day.

"What do you have to say to Eliakim?" she asked quickly.

"Don't call him Eliakim, mother," I replied. "Remember, he must be called Jehoiakim by everyone. That was Pharaoh Neco's way of testing his faithfulness. The king has announced that we have just two weeks to get used to it. Anyone calling him Eliakim after that time will be punished – and one week has already gone. Be careful."

"I'll be careful, Jeremiah," she confirmed, "but what do you have to say to him?"

I told her the words Yahweh had spoken, reading them as glowing words in my mind. They were more gentle than those I had often spoken to Josiah.

"I will be careful to say 'Jehoiakim', but you need to be careful too," my mother said earnestly. "You know what he is like. If God has told you what to say then you have no choice about that, but at least be careful how you say it. King Josiah is not there to protect you any more."

"Don't worry, Yahweh will protect me as he has promised," I responded, trying to sound supremely confident. My mother knew of God's promise to make me like a fortified city in the face of opposition – a city that my enemies could not overcome.[65]

Shortly after the meal I left for Jerusalem, hurrying across the familiar hillsides and cresting the gap south of Har Hatsophim. It was still early morning and I was alone on the path as the summer sun began to spread its heat over the land.

The gates were open when I arrived and a few guards sat just inside the entrance. I had already heard a report that the number of guards on duty at the city gates had been reduced, and it was noticeably true. Apparently, Pharaoh Neco had placed limits on the number of guards and soldiers which could be maintained. The guards who were on duty knew me well but asked my business as I approached. When I told them I had come to give King Jehoiakim a message from Yahweh, they looked at each other and smiled a little.

"Good luck!" one of the guards said.

"If you do things like that, don't be too surprised if you have to pay an entry fee next time you come," said another with a dry smile.

They waved me on and I walked into the city past the market area where sellers and buyers were already exchanging goods for money and sharing the latest gossip.

Making my way to the palace, I approached the guards at the gate and asked about Jehoiakim: how soon could I arrange an interview with the king?

"An interview with the king?" repeated one of the guards, looking at another, older, guard with a bit of a grin.

---

[65] Jeremiah 1:18-19

"The new king's not an early riser," said the older guard, whom I recognised. "There have been some changes around here since The Disaster," he added sadly.

"Interviews with the king are not so easy to arrange now," said the other guard, "and never before noon."

"I can wait," I conceded, "but I must see him."

"You're Jeremiah the prophet, aren't you?" asked the older guard, and I acknowledged the fact. "We'll pass on the message. You're not likely to get an answer today, though."

"If you were selling wine you might get an audience more quickly," chuckled the younger guard, "but then – you mightn't get paid for it anyway," he finished, the smile leaving his face.

I was amazed at the changes that were already so obvious in Jerusalem. Josiah's guards had always been serious and sober, and they had always shown their master complete respect. None of his guards would ever have spoken of him in this half-joking, half-contemptuous way.

After advising the guards that I would return at noon to see whether anything further could be arranged, I went to visit Zaccai. I had not spoken to him since the death of Josiah, although I had heard that he had been removed from his position, along with most of the advisors and administrators employed by Josiah.

Ahikam had told me that Josiah's most senior advisors were unlikely to ever be approached by Jehoiakim, but that less senior advisors and competent civic administrators would probably be employed again – given time. Jehoiakim did not want Judah to continue as it had been under the reign of his father, but he did like his comfort. Efficient and skilful leaders would be needed to run the kingdom in such a way that Jehoiakim could maintain this comfort. He might not like their closeness to his father, but his selfishness would drive him to use their skills anyway.

When I arrived at his door, Zaccai came quickly to welcome me. At that time he was unemployed, but he was in no danger of starving. His ancestral lands were south of Jerusalem and he controlled several other farms in the area as well. He also owned a few houses in Jerusalem, and was using his unexpected spare time to increase the returns he was earning on these properties. He expected to do quite well out of the change of focus, but he was still concerned about the future.

Prophets were the cause of this concern: Zephaniah his relative, Huldah the prophetess and I had all made prophecies that concerned him and made investment decisions difficult. Another prophet, Uriah, had also made prophecies during the last few years of Josiah's reign which had concentrated on the coming judgement on Jerusalem, the temple and the palace. He was an honourable and righteous man, though a little timid. Uriah and I had become close friends, and Zaccai had heard prophecies of destruction from both of us.

Although Zaccai would never have said so, he was convinced that our prophecies of destruction employed hyperbole as well as truth. Like many others, he could not really accept that Jerusalem would burn and its people die in terror.

His oldest son Daniel was an outstanding lad, about twelve or thirteen years of age at the start of Jehoiakim's reign. Very intelligent and mature for his age, he was also very godly. He had a good knowledge of God's law and put it into practice with courage and determination. Zaccai told me that Daniel had a few friends who were cast in the same sort of mould, and once again, my optimism almost got the better of me. Maybe there could be many more like him… but it was never a real possibility.

That morning we spoke together about the tragedy of Josiah's death and the changes that were already overtaking the kingdom. Daniel was with us and mostly listened in silence, but from time to time his father asked him questions directly. His answers reminded me a lot of Ahikam, except that they always seemed to spring from a stronger base of "Yahweh says…."

When I left to press my demands for an audience with the king, I carried the hope that in five or ten years Daniel would be able to take an important place among the leadership of Judah. But God had other plans for Daniel and no plans to bless the declining star of Judah.

☙

King Jehoiakim took the opportunity to show me that he was not eager to hear the word of Yahweh. It was four days before he would deign to see me and when he did so, he had prepared his defences. I was offered, not a private audience, but only an opportunity to speak during one of the king's judgement sessions, which were often held in public at the gate of the palace.

As I waited my turn, I watched King Jehoiakim, dressed as usual in expensive imported clothes, sitting casually on a raised throne chatting to his young friends seated on either side of the throne. Some were there as appointed advisors, but others were just there to provide entertainment and emotional support. Looking around at this group made me feel a little old: they were all under thirty.

I stood in a small crowd of those who were waiting for their cases to be processed, surrounded by a larger crowd of those who liked to watch judgement being meted out.

Standing off to one side was another group of men, some of whom I recognised as popular false prophets. These were men who had previously argued with me about God's word, ridiculed me and made counter-prophecies. Whereas I warned the people about God's coming judgement, they promoted a message that God would not judge, but would always bless. For them, the main message of scripture was that God had chosen the people of Israel and that Jerusalem was, and would forever be, his home.

There was a wide spread of religious opinion amongst them, but overall they maintained that God's laws had been twisted and misapplied by zealots like me who wanted to keep people from enjoying life. According to them, God was simply a gentle and friendly old man who liked nothing more than to see his creation having fun. Commands were construed as wise advice for those who chose to follow them, and any apparent condemnation of idol worship or immoral behaviour was merely people misunderstanding the intent of the text. Naturally, these men were sure that they knew what the intent of the text was, and it never seemed to match what the text actually said. Each of them did and said what he thought was right.

Some of them were powerful orators, and they did their best to paint genuine prophets as bigoted killjoys. I had been their target on many occasions in the past, though normally outside Jerusalem, away from the influence of King Josiah. But King Josiah's death had removed the restraining hand of godliness and these men had begun to attack with new vigour and confidence. I guessed that they had been brought together today to help King Jehoiakim put me in my place.

After a few cases had been considered briefly, the guards announced me. As I walked forward, Jehoiakim looked at me with a sardonic smile. Clearly he felt that his preparations would be a surprise to me and catch me on the back foot.

"Ah, here comes Jeremiah the man of gloom," said the king. "What burdens do you have for us today?"

His friends turned to look at each other and sniggered. The assembled prophets also smiled in a self-satisfied way.

"I have a message for you from Yahweh, the living God who does not change; who speaks and brings it to pass," I answered in a loud voice. When people are ridiculing you or your words, it is hard to know quite how to handle it. From experience, I have found that staying serious generally gets the best results, but even so, the results are not always good.

"Should we hear his words?" asked Jehoiakim of his advisors.

"Has not the nation heard them all through the reign of your honoured father?" asked Jaazaniah the son of Azzur, who was sitting on Jehoiakim's right.

"But if we hear them in this new time, we can weigh what he says," argued Elnathan the son of Achbor.

The advisors argued back and forth, but eventually it was agreed that I should be given a chance to speak, and that what I said could be used to decide whether or not I would have any further opportunity to speak to the king.

"Speak," said the king.

So I spoke the words God had directed me to say:

" 'Hear the word of the Lord, O king of Judah,
who sits on the throne of David,
you, and your servants,
and your people who enter these gates.
Thus says the Lord:
Do justice and righteousness,
and deliver from the hand of the oppressor
him who has been robbed.
And do no wrong or violence to the resident alien,

the fatherless, and the widow,
nor shed innocent blood in this place.' "[66]

These words were followed by God's promise that if these principles were followed, the kingdom of Judah would continue, but that ignoring them would bring desolation to palace and city alike.

After I had finished, there was silence in the gate for a few seconds. Some of the audience looked a little shocked by the blunt threat of destruction with which God's words concluded. King Jehoiakim did not look pleased.

After a while, he spoke: "Jeremiah, your words are always threatening and depressing, always interfering with the lives of others. When will you bring good news?"

"The good news is up to you, O king," I replied. "Do justice and righteousness and the line of David will continue to rule. If there is bad news, you alone have chosen it."

"Take care what you say to the king, prophet," said the guard closest to me, threateningly. I ignored him and continued to look at the king, hoping that somehow he would listen and change. He was a son of Josiah – surely he must have some good in him.

One of the so-called prophets stepped forward. "My lord," he said, bowing to the king, "may I speak?"

King Jehoiakim gave him permission and he began: "When a prophet speaks he can be tested by the words he speaks. If his words come to pass, he can be trusted and we should listen to every word he speaks. Jeremiah has now been prophesying for almost twenty years. Twenty years! And how many of his prophecies have come true? He speaks of doom and destruction, but how many of his words have come to pass? The only disaster that has come

---

[66] Jeremiah 22:2-3

is the death of your revered father, who tried to follow the instructions of this charlatan."

"Your words make sense," responded King Jehoiakim; "much more sense than those of Jeremiah." He turned to me and continued, "Jeremiah, son of Hilkiah, why should we listen to you? You say disaster will come, but it never does. Everything continues as it always has and your warnings come to nothing. Why should we let you speak any more?"

"My lord, O king," I replied, "Yahweh promised that destruction would not come in the time of your father and it didn't. Even now, God is giving you an opportunity to avoid this devastating invasion from the north. But if you ignore God's commands, the invasion will surely come."

Jehoiakim looked across at the group of prophets, obviously expecting them to answer my words, and their leader didn't disappoint him. "O king, again Jeremiah speaks of the future, always the future, putting off the time when his credibility as a prophet can be tested. The man is a fraud and an embarrassment to his family. He is a priest too, from Anathoth, but the priests also find him an embarrassment. No-one wants to hear what he says, no-one believes what he says, but no-one dares to take any steps to silence him. If only the citizens of Anathoth would do so, while they still have any credibility in the sight of my lord!"

I was given no opportunity to respond to this attack and was dismissed within a few minutes. In the expansive mercy of God, Jehoiakim had been shown the way of life, and offered a choice between it and the way of death. He had chosen the way of death, and hundreds of thousands would die because of that choice.

Chapter 8

Violence

Shortly after my interview with Jehoiakim, the summer ended and I survived the first serious plot to kill me. I might never have known anything about it until it was too late, except that Yahweh made it known to me.[67]

I was not on the roster of priests to work in the temple again until the feasts of the seventh month, so I planned to spend the preceding month in Anathoth. It may have been the suggestion made before King Jehoiakim that the men of Anathoth should do something to silence me, but whatever it was, they had laid their plans against me.

The harvest of summer figs was coming to an end. Some of this fruit is dried and kept in the form of fig-cakes, which last much longer than fresh figs and provide a delicious snack as well.

I was rich enough to be able to live a life of idleness when I chose, but idleness achieves little and I had been

---

[67] Jeremiah 11:18-23 records a little information about the plot. Try reading it after finishing this chapter!

helping some family friends with spreading and later collecting their drying figs. One day, my childhood friend Chelub had approached me and asked if I could help with his figs. We had been estranged since the incident when I had destroyed the shrine of an idol on the hillside opposite Anathoth in the eighteenth year of King Josiah[68] and I had seen this as an opportunity to renew our acquaintance, in the hope of encouraging him in the worship of Yahweh. I was to go and assist him the next morning.

The night was warm and clear, but I had a disturbed sleep. Towards dawn, God showed me the plans of some men of Anathoth. It may have been a dream or it may have been a vision, I'm still not really sure. I felt that I had been awake before it started, but sleep can come and go without us having a clear view of its boundaries. I was certainly awake afterwards, but it may have been the shock of a horrible dream that woke me.

Anyway, whether through dream or vision, God showed me their schemes and their deeds. He showed them to me, plotting together as they planned to kill me. And I saw their faces and recognised them. One of the men – whom I could not see clearly enough to recognise until much later in the vision – was my former friend Benaiah, and the shock of that discovery has remained with me ever since, despite the years that have passed.

At first, I saw five men sitting around a table, talking. The faces of three I could see and recognise, but those of the other two were hidden from me.

"Let us destroy the tree with its fruit," said one of the men whom I could see. He lived a short way from us along the main street of Anathoth.

---

[68] See Volume 2 – As Good As It Gets, Chapters 3, 7 and 8.

"Let us cut him off from the land of the living," said the next, another man from Anathoth who lived a little way down the hill from us.

The words didn't make much sense, couched in symbols as they were, but the tone of their voices was threatening.

Their discussions continued, and it soon became clear that they were planning to entice someone into a trap. Murder was in their eyes. The two men whose faces I could not see contributed to the plotting, suggesting how the victim could be lured into a trap, tricked into accompanying them to a quiet place just outside Anathoth where they could all set upon him together. He would be led like a gentle lamb to the slaughter, unaware until the fatal stroke spilled his lifeblood on the ground.

As a helpless observer, I watched with growing horror, powerless to intervene: certain that this was significant, but unsure of what could be done.

"Let us cut him off from the land of the living," said the first speaker, "that his name be remembered no more." His words were so poetic, but utterly brutal.

"Let's wait no longer. Today must be the day!" said one of the men whose faces I could not see. I felt that I should know the voice, but I couldn't quite place its owner.

"Yes, he must die today," concluded the other man whose face I could not see.

I couldn't really believe what my eyes and ears were telling me. It must be a nightmare from which I would soon wake – but it was at this point that I became certain that I was awake, and still the scene continued to unfold. The five conspirators planned all the details of their scheme before parting.

Who were they planning to kill, I wondered?

The scene changed and I saw the main street of Anathoth. I knew that it was morning, and saw a man who looked vaguely familiar. I was looking from behind, so I could not see his face as he walked along the path until he met a man whom I recognised as Chelub, my erstwhile friend, and greeted him. My confusion continued to increase: Chelub had not been one of the five plotters, so how was he involved in this vision? The pair talked together as they walked towards the outskirts of Anathoth and along a small path that led down around a corner of the hill and beside a rocky cliff. Shrubbery and small trees grew close by the path.

As I watched, they followed the path between two large boulders. From my vantage point, I could see three men hiding in ambush behind the boulder on the left while another two were skulking on top of the boulder on the right. All five were armed with heavy clubs while two also carried gleaming blades, ready to strike.

I tried desperately to shout, to warn this innocent victim of his peril, but it was only a vision, and I could make no sound, nor convey any warning.

Chelub walked quickly between the massive rocks and hurried a short way past before turning and stopping his companion with a raised hand. The hapless victim was a step or two past the boulders, but stopped at Chelub's bidding. As he did so, the three men hidden behind the boulder leapt silently out swinging their heavy clubs. The victim may have heard a faint sound, because he half-turned before the first club struck him a vicious blow on the head and he dropped like a stone, face-first to the ground. All three of his assailants stood over him and rained down blows upon him. Down from their boulder slid the other two attackers and the leader abandoned his club as he reached the ground. Brandishing a long-bladed knife instead, he shouted as he ran the last few steps that separated him from the bundle of clothes lying on the ground. The other conspirators paused in their barrage of blows, as, dropping to his knees, he plunged his knife into the back of the unmoving body. Silence and stillness reigned for a time, then he rose to his feet and all five slowly stepped back to survey the results of their frenzied brutality.

A dusty pile of clothing lay alone in the middle of the path. The knife hilt protruded motionless in mute testament to the savage end it had brought to life.

I had watched the finale in utter horror, unable to comprehend what I was seeing. At some stage I had sat up, and my hands were shaking in shock, but still the vision was not finished. The man who had wielded the knife – I could now see that it was Benaiah, my friend – stepped forward again, gripped the shoulder of the corpse and tried to turn it over. The knife made it difficult, but he half-turned the body, looked down and laughed. "He won't tell us what to do anymore, will he?"

At that point, the vision ended abruptly and the voice of God spoke gently:

"These are the plans they have made against you,
    but now you know how to avoid them."

The shock was beyond description. I had made an arrangement to meet Chelub this very morning. Was this their plan for today?

I felt like a gentle lamb being led to the slaughter.

And then anger and fear overcame me and I spoke to God about my people as I had never done before: "O Lord of hosts, who judges righteously, who tests the heart and the mind, let me see your vengeance upon them, for to you have I committed my cause."

God's reply was immediate:

"Behold, I will punish them.
The young men shall die by the sword,

their sons and their daughters shall die by famine,
and none of them shall be left.
For I will bring disaster upon the men of Anathoth,
the year of their punishment."[69]

☙

February, 608 BC – the 1st year of King Jehoiakim

Life is precious, but constant, carping criticism and relentless opposition make life hard. Knowing that people were making plans to kill me made life harder than ever. God had protected me, shown me their plans, and given me the knowledge I needed to avoid the terror that surrounded me – but knowing that people hate you so much makes joy difficult.

Manasseh's goals for Judah had regained sharp focus after a brief reprieve: Josiah was gone and a final darkness was falling on the nation.

Worse was yet to come, and within months the signs were clear.

Another prophet who spoke the words of God in Jerusalem at that time was Uriah the son of Shemaiah. He was originally from Kiriath-jearim, a town about half a day's journey west of Jerusalem.[70] I had first met him in Kiriath-jearim early in my career as a prophet during one of my tours around Israel and Judah, when God had sent me to speak his words to all the people. He was one of the few who had listened to God's words and taken notice. Over the years we had become friends as we met in my travels around Judah and at the three annual feasts in Jerusalem. Later in the reign of Josiah, God had spoken

---

[69] Jeremiah 11:22-23
[70] Kiriath-jearim is about 10km (7 miles) west-northwest of Jerusalem as the crow flies.

to him occasionally through dreams and visions, but his main task as a prophet came early in the reign of King Jehoiakim, shortly after my unpleasant experience at the king's gate. Through a dream, God gave him words that foretold disaster for Jerusalem and the temple.

Following God's directions, after speaking these words in Kiriath-jearim, Uriah repeated them in Jerusalem itself at the gates of the temple. As he was speaking, the king passed by with some of his officials and the leaders of the army. Jehoiakim didn't stop to listen, of course – that would have been beneath him – but he heard enough to pique his interest and directed one of his nobles and one of the army chiefs to stay and determine the import of the message.

Uriah spoke well, and as I listened, God's words in his mouth caused me to examine my own life to see how well it was aligned with the behaviour God demanded. But King Jehoiakim's representatives didn't seem to be affected in the same way. Threats of punishment from God, including the demolition of city and temple, seemed only to inspire anger in them. They listened to the end, then enquired of the bystanders for Uriah's name and the details of what had been said before they arrived. All in all, they made it very clear that this was an official investigation and that serious charges against Uriah might easily result. Protestations that these were the words of Yahweh and spoken at his direction made no difference – Jehoiakim's men would not listen to us.

Once they had gone, Uriah and I spoke together. He was not an assertive or particularly courageous man, so it had taken all his nerve to come to Jerusalem and do as God commanded. And now this – threats of an investigation and possible punishment from the king. We talked for some time and I did my best to encourage him with the guarantee of protection that God had given me. But he hadn't been given any such guarantee, and his courage was failing him. Should he go back to Kiriath-jearim immediately?

As we continued to discuss the matter, Elnathan the son of Achbor appeared. Achbor had been one of the "six mysterious men" I had encountered during my first round of prophesying in Jerusalem[71] and his son Elnathan was continuing the family tradition of working in the king's household. He was one of a small group of nobles who were trying to limit Jehoiakim's excesses, though with little success.

"Jeremiah," he said to me, "apparently, there was a prophet speaking to the crowd here a short time ago. Is this the man?"

"Yes, Elnathan," I replied, "this is Uriah, a prophet of Yahweh. Why do you ask?"

"King Jehoiakim sent me to find out more about him: where he comes from, his family and his authority to speak the words he was speaking."

Elnathan was dressed in the fine clothes you would expect to see on a rich nobleman, while Uriah was dressed in the plain and simple clothes you would expect of a common man of the countryside. He also treated Uriah in the way you might expect, showing little respect and demanding immediate, detailed answers. Uriah answered each question carefully, looking more and more worried as the interrogation proceeded. Had I known all of what would follow, I might have tried to intervene more to support him.

Elnathan soon finished his questions, and left after saying, "I'll have to report back to the king. He was saying that he thought you deserved to die, but I don't think he was completely serious. However, it did sound as if he might lock you up or punish you. Words like those you

---

[71] See Volume 1 – Early Days, Chapters 4-9.

spoke threaten the entire kingdom, and you don't seem have any valid authority to speak – unlike Jeremiah here, you're not even a priest or a Levite."

"But Yahweh's command is the best authority anyone can have for anything," I protested.

"You tell the king that," retorted Elnathan. "Well, I'll just have to go and report all this."

He walked away and Uriah watched him go with fear in his eyes.

"Deserve to die!" he repeated shrilly, looking at me and shaking his head. "Just for speaking the words of Yahweh?"

What could I say? I agreed with Elnathan that it was unlikely that Jehoiakim was serious, and believed that if Uriah stood firm and continued to announce God's words, God would protect him. But though I tried to convince him, fear had overwhelmed him. When we parted that afternoon, he was planning to return immediately to Kiriath-jearim.

☙

Uriah didn't stay in Kiriath-jearim. His fear prompted him to flee to Egypt early the next day, and he left none too soon.

Elnathan had reported to King Jehoiakim the results of his questioning of Uriah, and the king had immediately ordered Uriah's arrest. Elnathan was told to take a few armed men and to find Uriah and bring him before the king, a task that proved long and arduous.

Investigations showed that Uriah had fled to Kiriath-jearim, so Elnathan and his men followed. But when they arrived in Kiriath-jearim, they learned that Uriah had already left, escaping to Egypt in fear of his life.

Elnathan returned to Jerusalem and reported the news to the king, expecting Jehoiakim to dismiss the matter from his mind, but he had underestimated the malice that brooded in Jehoiakim's heart.

"If he's run away to Egypt," he snarled, "then go there and seize him and bring him back. He deserves to be punished."

After it was all over, Elnathan told me that he had never before seen the king look so determined, and had hurried to depart. Taking with him his armed men and two friends, he had made his way to Egypt, quickly picking up the trail of Uriah, who was moving swiftly but not hiding his route. Clearly, he had not expected anyone to follow him.

Two weeks later, Elnathan had arrived in Egypt and visited Pharaoh Neco's palace, trying to arrange for the extradition of a citizen of Judah who was wanted in Jerusalem for crimes against King Jehoiakim. Some time was spent waiting, but when an interview was finally granted, Pharaoh Neco's representatives had agreed readily enough. They had even helped Elnathan's armed men to arrest Uriah and bind him in chains for the journey back from Egypt. Before Elnathan left, though, Pharaoh had given him a brief note for King Jehoiakim.

At that stage, Elnathan had been convinced that Uriah would probably just be beaten and locked up for a while. He told me that he had not been completely in favour of that, but had argued that people who speak against the state sometimes have to suffer for it.

After making the long trek back to Judah, Uriah was locked up in the king's prison. Three days later, Jehoiakim was finally ready to see him and he was called before the king, still in chains.

Some of Jehoiakim's advisors were there with the king, and four guards brought in Uriah. Elnathan described to the king how Uriah had been taken prisoner without resistance and reported that Pharaoh Neco had sent a message which had now been translated into Hebrew. Would the king like to hear the message?

"Yes," replied Jehoiakim, eagerly.

Elnathan answered, "It says:

'Pharaoh Neco to Jehoiakim of Judah,

Greetings.

As requested, we have provided assistance in the apprehension and detention of an escaped criminal from Judah. The said criminal was entrusted to the care of Elnathan, the son of Achbor, your delegate in this matter.

We trust that, as our appointed representative over the kingdom of Judah, your law enforcement efforts will in future be adequate to ensure that such criminals do not escape from the area placed under your supervision.' "

Elnathan looked up at the king and saw uncontrolled fury burning in Jehoiakim's eyes as his fingers drummed on the arms of his throne. Haltingly, Elnathan continued, "Pharaoh ends with a normal formal conclusion. That is all."

Jehoiakim raised his right fist and pounded it angrily on the armrest. Pharaoh Neco's comments reflected on his ability to control his kingdom, and he was sure it was all Uriah's fault. He stood and strode towards Uriah and the guards who had brought him in. "Give me your sword." The words were spat out at one of the guards as Jehoiakim held out his hand. The guard looked surprised, but grasped the hilt of his sword and eased it from the scabbard. Holding the blade carefully, he offered the hilt to Jehoiakim, who seized it impatiently.

"Now, you fool of a prophet," shouted Jehoiakim, "your words and your cowardly actions deserve death, and I am going to give it to you!"

He stepped closer to Uriah, swung the sword up over his head and struck him down. Blow after blow followed until there was no doubt that Uriah was dead.

Chapter 9

Clay or stone?

April, 608 BC – the 1st year of King Jehoiakim

I defy any human being to be as patient as Yahweh our God.

Without question, God loves his prophets, but there had been plots against me and the brutal murder of my friend Uriah in swift succession – and still God was warning his nation instead of punishing them.

Uriah was not long dead when God spoke to me as I rested on my bed in the heat of the day. I was on duty in the temple that day and had been about to rise and return to my work. But this occasion marked a change in my directions from God. Until then, there had never been a command for immediate action that had taken me away from my appointed work in the temple, but from that day on, things were different.

Once again, God's fire spread through me and his word followed:

> "Arise, and go down to the potter's house,
> and there I will let you hear my words."[72]

Immediately, I rose and went to the Potsherd Gate. I had a slight acquaintance with one of the potters who worked there, a man who had produced much of the pottery we had used in the High Priest's house in Jerusalem while my father was alive. He was an old and skilful worker, and I had continued to buy pottery from him since, whenever I needed any.

I haven't always been able to understand God's instructions immediately, and on that occasion, I had no idea why he wanted me to go to the potter's house or what I should do once I got there – but of course, I went anyway. When I arrived, the potter was working at the wheel in his house, forming a pot.

"I'll be finished in a few moments," he called when he saw me.

Unsure of what God had planned for me, I simply stood and watched in fascination as he worked. The spinning pot took shape rapidly under his skilful fingers, its delicate curved rim rising quickly as the fine clay was drawn upward, deftly pressed and formed, compelled to take the profile chosen by the potter. This was to be a piece of elegant, expensive pottery. Under the gentle insistence of his dextrous, coordinated movements, the clay became thinner and smoother. To my inexpert eye, all seemed to be going well, but the potter was not pleased. He stopped the wheel and examined the pot closely, then shook his head and remarked: "Some impurities in the clay. It will not turn out as I wanted. I must start again – do you mind waiting?"

Since I still did not know what I had come for, I assured him that I was happy to wait, and he began again. The pot was squeezed again into a lump of clay, and this

---

[72] Jeremiah 18:2

time the potter formed it into a less exquisite pot with thicker walls where the imperfections would matter less.

Suddenly, the fire spread through me again, and clay, wheel and potter went dim before my eyes as God's words came:

> "O house of Israel, can I not do with you
> as this potter has done? declares the Lord.
> Behold, like the clay in the potter's hand,
> so are you in my hand, O house of Israel.
> If at any time I declare
> concerning a nation or a kingdom,
> that I will pluck up and break down and destroy it,
> and if that nation, concerning which I have spoken,
> turns from its evil,
> I will relent of the disaster that I intended to do to it."[73]

See what patience God has, and how forgiving he is if people will only repent! At the same time, God also went on to make it clear that the reverse is true too: a promised blessing will be cancelled if the person's behaviour changes so that it no longer warrants the blessing. But though that part was very important for reminding righteous people to maintain their righteousness, it was irrelevant for the nation of Judah as a whole. For them, God continued with the words:

> "Now, therefore, say to the men of Judah
> and the inhabitants of Jerusalem: 'Thus says the Lord,
> Behold, I am shaping disaster against you
> and devising a plan against you.
> Return, every one from his evil way,
> and amend your ways and your deeds.' "[74]

I do not have the same patience as God, and answered him, "But they say, 'That is in vain! We will follow our own

---

[73] Jeremiah 18:6-8
[74] Jeremiah 18:11

plans, and will every one act according to the stubbornness of his evil heart.' "[75]

"Therefore thus says the Lord:
Ask among the nations, who has heard the like of this?
The virgin Israel has done a very horrible thing.[76]

"Like the east wind I will scatter them before the enemy.
I will show them my back, not my face,
in the day of their calamity."[77]

God's words had finished and the fire within drove me to action. I had a new message to announce to the nation, and I left the potter's house immediately. By this time, I could be almost certain that the response of my audience would be negative, possibly violent and probably dangerous; nevertheless, the message had to be given. The urge to act was irresistible.

Over the next few days, I publicly announced God's words at several of the gates of Jerusalem and some of the larger towns of Judah. On God's behalf, I demanded repentance, and promised defeat at the hands of their enemies and hostility from God if they did not obey.

Did anyone listen? I don't know for sure, but I don't think so. Some made threats of violence and many openly ridiculed the idea that Jerusalem and the temple could ever be destroyed. I even began to hear people telling stories about me – mere rumours and gossip, really – that attacked my integrity. In one town, I heard a conversation that seemed to sum up the universal attitude.

"Come, let us make plots against Jeremiah, for the law shall not perish from the priest," said one man.

---

[75] Jeremiah 18:12
[76] Jeremiah 18:13
[77] Jeremiah 18:17

"No, nor counsel from the wise, nor the word from the prophet," answered his companion.

"Come, let us strike him with the tongue," continued the first, "and let us not pay attention to any of his words."[78]

I had had enough. Although nobody had actually done anything to me, I felt that it was probably just a matter of time. In those frightening days, God's promise of protection slipped from my mind, and I became angry and fearful. Returning to Anathoth, I mulled over my misfortune in being a prophet and the injustices I was suffering.

In my self-pity, I prayed to God and reminded him of the intercession I had made for my people – until he had told me to stop: "Hear me, O Lord, and listen to the voice of my adversaries. Should good be repaid with evil? Yet they have dug a pit for my life. Remember how I stood before you to speak good for them, to turn away your wrath from them."[79]

It seemed completely unfair, and I didn't just want their hatred to stop, I wanted God to punish them for it. For the first time, I asked God to do the things he had been threatening against Judah throughout my career as a prophet: "Therefore deliver up their children to famine; give them over to the power of the sword; let their wives become childless and widowed. May their men meet death by pestilence, their youths be struck down by the sword in battle."[80]

It was not to be long before God started to answer my prayer, but before then, I was to suffer some of the troubles I had feared.

---

[78] Jeremiah 18:18
[79] Jeremiah 18:19-20
[80] Jeremiah 18:21

℘

> "Thus says the Lord:
> Stand in the court of the Lord's house,
> and speak to all the cities of Judah
> that come to worship in the house of the Lord
> all the words that I command you to speak to them;
> do not hold back a word.
> It may be they will listen,
> and every one turn from his evil way,
> that I may relent of the disaster
> that I intend to do to them because of their evil deeds.
> You shall say to them,
> 'Thus says the Lord: If you will not listen to me,
> to walk in my law that I have set before you,
> and to listen to the words of my servants the prophets
> whom I send to you urgently,
> though you have not listened,
> then I will make this house like Shiloh,
> and I will make this city a curse
> for all the nations of the earth.' "[81]

These were the words that God wrote in fiery letters on the wall of my mind one morning as I walked through the gates of the temple. I had been rostered on duty in the temple that day, but this changed my duty: instead of the leading priests deciding my tasks in the house of God, the owner of the house himself was setting the terms.

Without realising it, I stopped in my tracks as God spoke. Apparently one of the gatekeepers greeted me, but I heard nothing of his greeting, and did not respond.

Soon the words had been delivered and the fire abated a little, but the urge to act was as strong as it had ever been. I walked into the temple court immediately to

---

[81] Jeremiah 26:2-6

obey. It is often better not to think too much about God's work. That way lies terror.

So I stood in the courts and told all the people there that I had words from God to speak and would deliver them soon. Others were passing through and I warned them too. By emphasising the importance of the words they would hear, I managed to convince quite a group to wait for the message. One or two of the other priests saw the gathering crowd and asked what was going on. When it was explained, they hurriedly called other priests. Not only that, but somehow, the professional prophets – prophets of Yahweh, supposedly – ended up in the assembly as well. I would have preferred them not to be there.

As the throng grew, I knew that what God had told me to say would be touching a raw nerve. The temple was an extra-special place, sacred for its own sake, not just because it was the house of God. According to the doctrine of the priests and all the people, Jerusalem could never be destroyed as Shiloh had been because God had put his name there forever. Its destruction was utterly unthinkable, and to suggest it was heresy.

But God had specified the words. Exactly. Not one was to be left out. The conflict could not be avoided.

Once the crowd was ready, I repeated the words God had specified, word by word. A crowd is like a living thing; it doesn't just behave like the people of whom it consists. Responses multiply and the throng feeds on its own reactions. Very early on, it was clear that I would be in trouble, and by the end, the trouble had already begun.

Angry faces surrounded me and shouting broke out. "Death" and "Kill him" were popular expressions, while the leading priests in the mob rushed towards me with their hands over their ears – until they took them away to grab me.

"You shall die!" they screamed at me, and their furious faces showed that they were completely serious.

Many of the priests, the prophets and the people would have liked to kill me immediately, and they probably would have done so except for God's hand restraining their madness. Inexplicably, they just held me and shouted for a while as someone went and fetched a few of the nobles who had chambers in the temple.

My life was saved by that delay, and by the words of the nobles, particularly Ahikam, the son of Shaphan.[82] They first won over the people, then calmed them using the example of Micah when he had prophesied to Hezekiah in the name of Yahweh. Hezekiah had listened to the prophet rather than killing him.

The entire crowd – even the nobles, I believe – completely disagreed with my words, but King Jehoiakim had not become involved and his brutal methods of dealing with opposition had not been used. Chance? Of course not. Yet again, God had saved me as he had promised, and the need to stand up against all opposition was brought to the forefront of my mind once more. If only Uriah could have been saved in the same way.

ॐ

God had shown me that pottery – before it was fired – could be reshaped, but was Judah really made of clay? My nation had a heart of stone: could it be reshaped?

---

[82] Jeremiah 26:24

Chapter 10

Patience ending

March, 606 BC – the 3rd year of King Jehoiakim

During the third year of King Jehoiakim, God spoke to me more often. The situation in Judah was worsening, with more and more people disappearing and never being seen again. Stories of cruelty and injustice became common and people feared any involvement with Jehoiakim's law enforcement. Judgement is not the same as justice.

At the same time, the people had also changed. Under King Josiah, the temple had been a popular place, important in the spiritual life of the nation – but even in those days, God had showed that he did not accept their worship as genuine or truly holy. Once Jehoiakim placed his stamp on the life of the nation, though, things became much worse.

God once told me to go through the streets of Jerusalem to see whether I could find anyone who did justice and looked for truth.[83]

I spent a month trying to find such a man in the city. I asked many of the common people to tell me anyone whom they considered righteous, and spent many hours searching out these people and speaking to them. God was right. At times, he helped me in my investigation of these so-called just people, showing me examples of their behaviour and helping me to understand exactly what they meant by their answers to my questions. It was a great shock to me, but I found that none of them knew what God's justice really was, and not one of them wanted to learn more about truth. Though there were some "nice" people who appeared to worship Yahweh in their own ways, not one of them wanted to listen humbly to God's words through Moses or David.

Then I responded to God that this was just the simple, poor, common people. Ignorant and uninformed, they could not really be expected to understand the ways of God as would the nobles with their better education, greater intelligence and wider experience.[84] So I began searching through the nobles, the wise and the intelligent, but I found that they had all broken away from God. Even my friends among the nobles had changed since the death of Josiah. Slowly but surely, they had come to see advantages in freedom from the laws of God.

For example, although Zaccai and Abigail were still enthusiastically godly in appearance, over recent years their riches had taken their focus away from God, particularly since Zaccai had lost his job as an advisor after the death of Josiah. There were numerous poor people living near their house, some of whom had no house of

---

[83] Jeremiah 5:1-2
[84] Jeremiah 5:4-5.

their own and lived in unused buildings or at the ends of narrow alleys. Many were willing to work, but the rich wanted exploitation, not fair work – virtual slavery was all they offered the poor. The numbers of such people had increased greatly since Josiah's demise, and I saw many children around the city in tattered clothes. Josiah had used his position to help people like that, and had stopped his nobles from oppressing them whenever he could.[85] King Josiah had read the Book of the Law and paid attention to such words as:

> " 'Cursed be anyone who perverts the justice due
> to the sojourner, the fatherless, and the widow.'
> And all the people shall say, 'Amen.' "[86]

Josiah had said "Amen" to these words, by obeying them, but nobody did now.

When I spoke to Zaccai about this poverty, he explained to me that such people did not live wisely, and that helping them by giving them work was wasted effort. They would not work well and would squander whatever wages or other help they received. I am sure that he was right in many cases, but Josiah had helped such people anyway, and God's laws made frequent reference to helping the poor and needy – whether their poverty was their own fault or not.

Ahikam, the son of Shaphan, was another candidate I considered, but I found that he was concentrating too much on his position and importance, as he was having to fight for recognition against the wilder and more undisciplined advisors often preferred by Jehoiakim. He was still a loyal and good friend, but God did not always seem to come first for him.

---

[85] Jeremiah 22:15-16; Zephaniah 1:8-9
[86] Deuteronomy 27:19

These were the better examples. The majority, rich and poor alike, were openly godless and immoral. None would listen to the word of Yahweh. Adultery and prostitution were growing problems.[87]

I did find a few individuals who seemed likely to follow justice and seek truth when they grew up, but who were still only youths: Daniel and his friends. A youth from a priestly family also came to my notice, Ezekiel the son of Buzi, who was about the same age as Daniel and showed similar promise. These boys were a pleasure to be with, as they looked to God for guidance rather than their own ambitions. They really were looking for truth and trying to be just in their ways. At the time, I hoped, a little doubtfully, that this would continue as they matured; happily, subsequent events have shown that it did.

To be honest, this investigation was actually a great help to me personally. It made me search my own motives and desires, and once again sharpened my determination for righteousness. From then on, I did my best to help the poor, the fatherless and widows, focusing on it as part of doing justice and seeking truth. There was no point in learning the faults of many others if I was unable to see my own and work to overcome them.

God gave me many words to speak to the people at that time, and told me that his words would be a fire in my mouth, and the people wood to burn,[88] but no-one listened. He expressed his fury at my nation, but also his resignation:

<blockquote>
"Shall I not punish them for these things?
declares the Lord,
and shall I not avenge myself on a nation such as this?
An appalling and horrible thing
has happened in the land:
</blockquote>

---

[87] Jeremiah 5:7-9
[88] Jeremiah 5:14

the prophets prophesy falsely,
and the priests rule at their direction;
my people love to have it so,
but what will you do when the end comes?"[89]

What a picture of hopelessness! Punishment would come, but would no-one believe it?

"To whom shall I speak and give warning, that they may hear?" I asked Yahweh. "Behold, their ears are uncircumcised, they cannot listen; behold, the word of the Lord is to them an object of scorn; they take no pleasure in it. Therefore I am full of the wrath of the Lord; I am weary of holding it in."[90]

And God replied:

" 'Pour it out upon the children in the street,
and upon the gatherings of young men, also;
both husband and wife shall be taken,
the elderly and the very aged.
Their houses shall be turned over to others,
their fields and wives together,
for I will stretch out my hand
against the inhabitants of the land,'
declares the Lord.
'For from the least to the greatest of them,
everyone is greedy for unjust gain;
and from prophet to priest, everyone deals falsely.
They have healed the wound of my people lightly,
saying, "Peace, peace," when there is no peace.' "[91]

God's patience was coming to an end. The time for action was near. God told me of a nation coming that was cruel and would not show mercy.[92] Their quiver, God

---

89 Jeremiah 5:29-31
90 Jeremiah 6:10-11
91 Jeremiah 6:11-14
92 Jeremiah 6:22-23

said, was an open tomb.[93] It was a terrifying picture – judgement was coming.

And now, probably because of my angry responses to my people's attitudes, God had another job for me:

"I have made you a tester of metals among my people,
that you may know and test their ways.
They are all stubbornly rebellious,
going about with slanders;
they are bronze and iron; all of them act corruptly."[94]

Somehow, I was to test my nation, assess their quality, review their behaviour, and decide whether they were good or bad. Yet God had described them as corrupt, so how could my assessment be otherwise?

God wanted me to test and judge my nation myself, not just to deliver messages from him. The messages had to be my messages also, the judgements mine, the condemnation mine. I had to own God's judgements. This was easy when I was angry, but much harder when talking to friends or watching children play on the streets.

And God would judge my judgements.

❧

I flung the earthenware flask to the ground where it shattered, spraying fragments across the roadway and among the listening elders grouped around me in the shadow of the Potsherd Gate. The crowd gasped and stepped back, some receiving stinging blows from pieces of fired clay as the pot exploded on the cobblestones.

"Thus says the Lord of hosts:" I shouted, " 'So will I break this people and this city, as one breaks a potter's vessel, so that it can never be mended.' " I waved my

---

[93] Jeremiah 5:16
[94] Jeremiah 6:27-28

hands at the shattered fragments strewn across the roadway, all that remained of the beautiful pot which I had carried so carefully to the Valley of Ben Hinnom – cursed Topheth – at the entrance to the Potsherd Gate.

" 'Men shall bury in Topheth because there will be no place else to bury,' " I continued. " 'Thus will I do to this place,' declares the Lord, 'and to its inhabitants, making this city like Topheth. The houses of Jerusalem and the houses of the kings of Judah – all the houses on whose roofs offerings have been offered to all the host of heaven, and drink offerings have been poured out to other gods – shall be defiled like the place of Topheth.' "[95]

God's words were ended and the crowd slowly dispersed. Yahweh had told me to call some of the elders of the people and of the priests, to bring them to this hated place and to condemn the worship of other gods and the offering of children as burnt offerings to Baal.[96] God's renaming of the valley as the Valley of Slaughter[97] had no impact. Punishment that related to a place outside the holy city brought no such indignant response as had met the words against the temple. I'm not sure where they thought all the dead bodies – enough to fill the valley – would be coming from. What did they think God meant by "and this city"? It seemed obvious to me that these would be the dead from the destruction of Jerusalem, but clearly my audience had not found that connection so obvious.

Of course, it is not that there was no response at all during my prophesying. There had been laughter – indeed, there seemed to have been laughter every time I had spoken for God since Jehoiakim became king. There had been complaints that I had brought them to Topheth

---

95 Jeremiah 19:11-13
96 Jeremiah 19:1-5
97 Jeremiah 19:6

to waste their time with the same pointless words that they had heard from me before. There had also been mocking and ridicule. I had invited Immer, my former teacher, to attend as an elder of the priests, and his nasal twang had rung out once during a pause in my message with the snide remark: "Aren't we lucky to have Jeremiah here to teach us these little lessons?" But there had been no anger, and definitely no humble admission of guilt.

So they trickled back into the city in twos and threes, discussing the words of God, probably happy that I wasn't talking about their temple or their city.

I left the shards of the beautiful flask scattered around and went on to the next part of my assignment. Next stop, the temple. This was to prove more dangerous.

CR

By the time I arrived at the temple that day, many of the elders who had gone to Topheth at my invitation had already returned there, and I heard my name mentioned in several of the animated conversations taking place within the temple courts. The earlier presentation of God's message as a living parable was being described with enthusiasm and plenty of waving arms, but with little respect for either the message or the messenger. Immer was there talking to his son Pashhur, who was now the chief officer of the temple,[98] responsible for the behaviour of visitors and their decorum within the sanctuary. When they saw me, both of them looked displeased.

I prepared to speak to the wide range of people who filled the temple courts, first finding a good place from which I would be able to be heard. An examination of the audience showed that neither of my brothers was anywhere in the courts – which I thought was probably a

---

[98] Jeremiah 20:1

good thing. Many antagonistic eyes were on me as I stood in my raised position.

"Thus says the Lord of hosts, the God of Israel," I called out in a loud voice, " 'behold, I am bringing upon this city and upon all its towns all the disaster that I have pronounced against it, because they have stiffened their neck, refusing to hear my words.' "[99]

You may think that this was nothing startling compared with many of the things God had previously told me to say, but it provoked the most spectacular response I ever received – and the most painful!

Pashhur instantly rushed at me with six other priests, shouting at me in anger. They grabbed my arms and hair and began to shake me, then pushed me over and dragged me along the pavement towards the upper Benjamin Gate of the temple. I struggled and squirmed, doing my best to regain my feet, but they wouldn't let me, and kept pushing me down again and kicking me. By the time we arrived at the gate, I was already rather bruised and scratched and my clothes were badly torn. Pashhur used his position as chief officer to immediately open a court of judgement, with the clear intention of having me beaten. Some of the men of Anathoth had planned this very thing for me in my early days as a prophet, but that time God had saved me through my mother's quick thinking, using the argument of King Josiah's condemnation of idols.[100] This time, the atmosphere of the nation was different – there was no King Josiah to provide godly leadership.

Pashhur opened the proceedings with the pompous statement that I was guilty of speaking against Jerusalem, the city in the which God had put his name forever. He asked for witnesses to this crime and all the priests who

---

[99] Jeremiah 19:15
[100] See Volume 2 – As Good As It Gets, Chapters 7 and 8.

had helped him confirmed his accusations. He announced that Jerusalem would be glorified in the future, not punished, and that my words should be ignored by all. My message was, he said, completely wrong and contrary to God's word.

There was little discussion and no defence was allowed.

The main topic of contention among the judges was whether I should be sentenced to time in the stocks as well as a whipping. They all agreed that everyone would consider the whipping a necessary punishment for my heinous crime.

Quickly wrapping up the discussion, Pashhur passed sentence on me: forty lashes[101] and one day in the stocks.

I stated as clearly as I could that these were the words of God and could not be dismissed so easily, but no-one was listening. Even as I spoke, Pashhur ordered me to be laid down on the ground and held there. The six priests who had helped him from the start threw me to the ground and held me forcibly while Pashhur tore the outer garment off my back. An assistant handed him the whip and Pashhur gave me forty lashes.

The pain was greater than I had ever experienced before, and grew even worse as Pashhur continued the brutal whipping. But it was the shock that struck me most. Surely God had promised that this would not happen to me? How could this be happening?

When the flogging finally finished, I was dragged over to the stocks and my feet were fastened in place. Pashhur inspected the stocks and assured himself that I could not escape. Immer looked at me and nodded a little, looking

---

[101] Jeremiah 20:2 speaks of "beating" while Deuteronomy 25:1-3 describes "stripes". This story assumes that the beating was given with a whip – as it seems to have been with Paul in 2 Corinthians 11:24-25.

quite satisfied. "So, your predictions of suffering have finally come true," he said. "Are you rejoicing?"

I didn't know what to say, so I said nothing. He looked at me sombrely and walked away.

All that evening and into the night I kept working on my problem as a dog gnaws on a bone. How could everything have gone so badly wrong? I complained to God and argued back and forth with myself.

"O Lord, you have deceived me, and I was deceived;" I complained, "you are stronger than I, and you have prevailed. I have become a laughingstock all the day; everyone mocks me. For whenever I speak, I cry out, I shout, 'Violence and destruction!' For the word of the Lord has become for me a reproach and derision all day long."[102]

I remembered the first time I had heard the words of God, when he told me that he had known me before he even formed me in the womb, and then described the job he had planned for me.

But he hadn't mentioned this! God had forced me to do what he wanted, and now I was a laughingstock and the butt of everyone's jokes. My complaints continued as darkness began to fall. The gates of the temple were locked and the gatekeeper walked past me, sneering, " 'The word of the Lord', 'the word of the Lord.' Maybe now we can have some peace from 'the word of the Lord.' "

He disappeared into his chamber and I was left alone, listening to the sounds of the city as everyone went to their homes and their families, gathering to eat their evening meals together.

---

[102] Jeremiah 20:7-8

"If I say, 'I will not mention him, or speak any more in his name,' there is in my heart as it were a burning fire shut up in my bones, and I am weary with holding it in, and I cannot."[103]

I tried to lie down, but, of course, my lacerated back wouldn't allow it. Somehow, I was going to have to stay sitting up all night. Even in the time of Josiah, being a prophet had been dangerous, but now King Josiah was gone and the list of my enemies just seemed to keep growing. Friends are meant to support each other when others attack. Instead, my close friends were the very ones who had started the attacks on me. And now it felt as if everyone was plotting against me.

"For I hear many whispering," I muttered. "Terror is on every side! 'Denounce him! Let us denounce him!' say all my close friends, watching for my fall. 'Perhaps he will be deceived; then we can overcome him and take our revenge on him.' "[104]

"But they haven't defeated me," I argued with myself.

"What do you call this, if it isn't defeat?" asked the little voice that is always there to argue against faith.

"I haven't given up yet, and I won't. The Lord is with me as a dread warrior; therefore my persecutors will stumble; they will not overcome me. They will be greatly shamed, for they will not succeed. Their eternal dishonour will never be forgotten. O Lord of hosts, who tests the righteous, who sees the heart and the mind, let me see your vengeance upon them, for to you have I committed my cause."[105]

In that hour after the sun had set, I longed for God to fulfil his promises of destruction. Gradually, though, I regained my balance and was able to relax a little and see

---

[103] Jeremiah 20:9
[104] Jeremiah 20:10
[105] Jeremiah 20:11-12

that God was keeping his promise to me. They hadn't prevailed against me. I could still continue, and God's prophecies would come true. As the moon rose, I was able to see the beauty of creation and thank God for the fact that I had not died as Uriah had. God had strengthened me, I was still alive, and I could still praise him.

"Sing to the Lord;" I said aloud, "praise the Lord! For he has delivered the life of the needy from the hand of evildoers."[106]

And in that upswing of confidence, I sang one of King David's Psalms of praise into the growing cold of night. But, oh dear, it was the wrong Psalm to choose! It had been one of my favourite Psalms in King Josiah's reign, starting with the rejoicing of the king in God's strength and his blessings.[107] It spoke of a king reigning in righteousness forever and of the defeat of his enemies – and suddenly all my hard-won confidence crumbled again. Josiah was dead. There was no king reigning in righteousness, no-one for whom God would deliver defeat to his enemies. Jehoiakim was no Josiah.

As darkness had fallen on me, locked in the stocks, so darkness was falling on Judah. For me, there was unmistakeable terror and hatred all around. Enemies attacked me, friends plotted against me, and even my brothers did not come to free me from my bondage or argue my innocence. My father himself had been my enemy to the day of his death. For Judah, the darkness would bring enemies and terror on every side, and there would be no escape – yet no-one seemed to recognise that the light was failing. I reached a very low ebb at that time, and spent some hours dwelling on my misery and how disastrous my life had become. I have always enjoyed poetry and written some from time to time. That night, I

---

[106] Jeremiah 20:13
[107] See Psalm 21.

passed some of my time of pain in composing a dirge of self-pity:

> "Cursed be the day on which I was born!
> The day when my mother bore me, let it not be blessed!
> Cursed be the man who brought the news to my father,
> 'A son is born to you,' making him very glad.
> Let that man be like the cities
> that the Lord overthrew without pity;
> let him hear a cry in the morning and an alarm at noon,
> because he did not kill me in the womb;
> so my mother would have been my grave,
> and her womb forever great.
> Why did I come out from the womb
> to see toil and sorrow,
> and spend my days in shame?"[108]

It was a very long night. A struggle of faith against doubt, of hope against despair, of purpose against uselessness. Pain was my constant companion and made rest impossible. The cold of the night bit into my bones and lowered my resistance even further. At times, I felt there was just no point in continuing: I had failed both as a man and as a prophet. But… I couldn't quite give up. I could not leave God.

Then, towards dawn, in the cold and friendless darkness, Yahweh spoke. For a time, the darkness disappeared and I felt completely surrounded by light and love. In the terrible hours of loneliness, I had made my choice, and the measureless love of my God was my reward. And how I needed it! I cannot express the words he said nor describe the depths of his gentleness and encouragement that completely blotted out the pain – for a time. God loved me. I didn't need any more encouragement to continue, but he gave it anyway, in the form of vindication. He gave me a message for Pashhur

---

[108] Jeremiah 20:14-18

my persecutor that I was to deliver when I was freed from the stocks.

Slowly the city awoke and the biting cold of night departed. The gates of city and temple alike were opened and I endured the last, most degrading phase of my current suffering. The stocks were placed near the gates of the temple so that anyone confined there was visible to all and a target for any who wanted one. I am not boasting when I say that I was well known in the city. Years of prophesying had meant that my face was recognised by many, and hated by most of those who recognised it. Many whose actions had been condemned by God's words bore a personal grudge against me and took with glee the opportunity to mock and ridicule me. At times that morning I had a crowd around me that was at least as large as those to which I had often prophesied. But this time I was their target. Some threw more than just insults, and I couldn't really dodge. The morning felt as long as the night had.

ʗʘ

During the afternoon, Pashhur finally came to release me from the stocks, accompanied by his two assistants. They freed me and I struggled to my feet, feeling quite dizzy and extremely tired.

"Jeremiah, go in peace," Pashhur said in a smooth voice, trying to make it sound as if I had forced him into a deed he had not wanted to do. "I hope that you have learned your lesson and will never again speak against God's holy city in that foolish way."

"The Lord does not call your name Pashhur, but *Terror on Every Side*," I replied. "For thus says the Lord: I will make you a terror to yourself and to all your friends."[109]

---

[109] Jeremiah 20:3-4

"Silence, you fool," Pashhur thundered. "I did not come to listen to your vacuous prophecies. Be silent and go – before you receive more punishment!"

But I could not be silent. "Your friends shall fall by the sword of their enemies while you look on," I continued, speaking God's words. "And I will give all Judah into the hand of the king of Babylon. He shall carry them captive to Babylon, and shall strike them down with the sword. I will give all the wealth of the city, all its gains, all its prized belongings, and all the treasures of the kings of Judah into the hand of their enemies, who shall plunder them and seize them and carry them to Babylon. And you, Pashhur, and all who dwell in your house, shall go into captivity. To Babylon you shall go, and there you shall die, and there you shall be buried, you and all your friends, to whom you have prophesied falsely."[110]

After his initial furious response, Pashhur stopped and listened to my words. All of them. He said no more and made no move to stop me.

As he had promised, God made sure that I was not defeated. His message had been delivered.

---

[110] Jeremiah 20:4-6

Chapter 11

A yoke for all

Jehoiakim had been king for about three years when God first named to me the nation that was to attack Judah and destroy Jerusalem. Throughout the reign of Josiah and the early years of Jehoiakim, God had spoken only of a destroyer from the north, a great nation from the furthest parts of the earth.[111]

More than one hundred years earlier, Isaiah the prophet had warned King Hezekiah that Babylon would attack Jerusalem one day and carry off its treasures and people. However, God had not previously made it clear that the time was fast approaching for Isaiah's prophecy to be fulfilled, and the details of Judah's fate had unfolded slowly. Being very familiar with the prophecies of Isaiah through reading my "smelly scroll"[112] so often, I had always considered it most likely that Babylon would be the nation that attacked from the north.

---

[111] Jeremiah 1:15; 4:6-7; 6:22
[112] See Volume 1 – Early Days, Chapter 12.

Now, Judah and the surrounding nations had gradually become aware of the threat of Babylon as an invading superpower. Assyria had lost its strength, and it had been confederations of Babylon and other nations that had destroyed their powerful citadels and overwhelmed their armies. Pharaoh Neco had ridden to the aid of Assyria in that terrible campaign when King Josiah had been killed, but that defeat had been only a temporary setback for Babylon. The very next year, the armies of Babylon had again taken the city of Haran in which the exiled king of Assyria had ruled, and his forces were gradually being driven back. It seemed likely that a final showdown was imminent, in which the dwindling kingdom of Assyria would be finally destroyed.

Yes, Babylon's power was growing, and our neighbours had begun to examine their options. Egypt was weakening, too, there was no doubt about it. No longer could she be relied on as a relatively benign superpower who would mostly leave her neighbours alone, while still providing a secure sphere of influence which would keep other superpowers at bay. Babylon was flourishing. She was sprouting branches and fruit, and her tendrils were slowly spreading and wrapping themselves around all the surrounding nations. The threat was real, and growing every day.

Of all of the smaller nations – Judah, Edom, Moab, Ammon, Tyre and Sidon – Judah was the most powerful. The other nations all hated her, but recognised her as a necessary partner in any coordinated defence against Babylon, if that proved necessary. Of course, Egypt still considered herself the mistress of these kingdoms and guardian of the area, so any regional discussions that excluded her could only be arranged with great caution. A low key gathering of envoys met in Jerusalem that autumn, knowing that Pharaoh Neco would not be pleased to hear of any conference being organised to discuss the Babylonian question.

While the envoys were in Jerusalem, making fruitless plans and offering grand-sounding commitments of unified support to repel the possible attackers, God gave me another task to fulfil.

> "Make yourself straps and yoke-bars,
> and put them on your neck.
> Send word to the king of Edom,
> the king of Moab, the king of the sons of Ammon,
> the king of Tyre, and the king of Sidon
> by the hand of the envoys
> who have come to Jerusalem."[113]

I am no carpenter, but we Levites do learn some whittling as part of our training in scribesmanship, and as a young lad I had enjoyed working with wood. However, it took me quite a long time to make such a yoke with bars and straps that would be strong enough and look realistic, so that I could wear it as I followed God's instructions. Since this yoke was meant to symbolise servitude, not the idea of two serving animals sharing a load, I started by forming a long wooden bar that sat across my shoulders behind my neck. Two shorter pieces of timber were attached to it, pointing forward, one on either side of my neck. A long strap was fixed to the two ends of the main bar, forming a loop behind my back.

For practical use, this loop would have been connected to a cart or whatever the poor victim had to

---

[113] Jeremiah 27:2-3. There is uncertainty about some details in this passage. Most Hebrew manuscripts say that this instruction came early in the reign of Jehoiakim, while verse 3 refers to King Zedekiah. The Septuagint gives no indication of who the king was, since it omits verse 1 completely and the name from verse 3. This story assumes that this episode took place early in the reign of King Jehoiakim, but that the same message was also delivered to Zedekiah when he became king (Jeremiah 27:12).

pull. Another strap was fastened across between the ends of the two short wooden bars that sat on either side of my neck to prevent the yoke from falling off as I walked around and spoke my message. It was rather late by the time I finished, so I had to wait until the next day for an opportunity to display my parable to the visiting dignitaries. Since I had no idea how long they might be staying, I knew that I needed to hurry in seeking them out.

I made sure that I got to the gate of the palace early the next morning. Although Jehoiakim was no early riser, I hoped that the visiting diplomats would use the hours of daylight more effectively.

As I arrived, a group of about fifteen men descended the steps from the palace and crossed the paved courtyard towards me. I recognised three of them as diplomats whom I had met when visiting Edom and Moab as part of my ongoing task as a prophet to the nations.

It was amazing. I had come early just in case, and now the very men I needed to speak to were walking straight out to meet me! I have already mentioned it several times in this diary, but it never ceases to amaze me how easily events normally work out when I do God's work immediately. At times, I have fought his will, and that is a recipe for lots of hard work. I always have to obey in the end, but if I resist it often takes so much longer to achieve and requires so much more effort than if I cooperate eagerly.

I must have looked strange with the yoke on my neck and my hands at either end of the cross bar, but the impression of servitude which a yoke gives is so strong that I don't believe any of the men would have looked at me or even noticed me if I had not hailed the men whose names I knew.

"Dishon, Ebal, Ithmah," I called, "Greetings, and welcome to Jerusalem."

Dishon and Ebal were both from Edom and they were the first to see me and respond. The Edomite language is very similar to Hebrew, so they were easily able to understand me, and recognised me after only a brief pause.

"Ah, Jeremiah, the prophet of Yahweh," said Dishon, the older of the two.

"And dressed up in a home-made yoke, no less," continued Ebal. Clearly my carpentry hadn't been as good as I thought.

I had wondered whether they would acknowledge or even remember me at all, but far from ignoring me, they walked towards me, smiling, and the other men followed them.

"Ah, now I recognise you," said Ithmah from Moab, the third man I had greeted. "I'm sorry but my eyes are failing me as I get older. Good health to you, Jeremiah." The Moabite language is also very similar to Hebrew and I had had no difficulty communicating with Ithmah in Moab.

"And good health to you," I replied.

The other men were looking a little bewildered, doubtless wondering why their colleagues were talking to this crazy-looking man wearing a home-made yoke!

"Why are you wearing a yoke, Jeremiah?" asked Dishon. "I thought you were a priest of Yahweh, not a slave."

"I am wearing the yoke because I am a prophet of Yahweh," I said, "and Yahweh has a message for the kings of all of the nations around."

"Is it the same message of destruction that you have given in the past?" enquired Ithmah. "Our king is worried enough about the possibility that he sent us here to try to arrange mutual support and cooperation against the threat of Chaldean hordes pouring down from the north."

"Well, this message is a little different, Ithmah," I observed. "I am to send a message through you envoys so that it will reach your kings. I know that we have representatives from Edom and Moab here, but what nations do you others represent?"

"Sidon," answered one.

"Good, good," I smiled.

"Ammon," added two more, in unison.

"Of course," I said with delight, "and…?"

"Tyre," answered a trio, standing together at the rear of the group.

"No more?" I asked, confident that there wouldn't be. There weren't. "Well, Yahweh told me to send the message to the kings of Edom, Moab, Ammon, Tyre and Sidon, and it sounds as if that's exactly the nations you all represent. Yahweh doesn't get things wrong, which is why you need to pay particular attention to this message from him:

" 'Thus says the Lord of hosts, the God of Israel:
This is what you shall say to your masters:
"It is I who by my great power
and my outstretched arm have made the earth,
with the men and animals that are on the earth,
and I give it to whomever it seems right to me.
Now I have given all these lands into the hand of
Nebuchadnezzar, the king of Babylon, my servant,
and I have given him also
the beasts of the field to serve him.
All the nations shall serve him
and his son and his grandson,
until the time of his own land comes.

Then many nations and great kings
shall make him their slave." ' "[114]

"Jeremiah," said Ebal from Edom, sardonically, "Your message sounds nice, but I'm afraid Nebuchadnezzar is not king of Babylon. Nabopolassar, his father, is king. Aren't you getting a bit mixed up?"[115]

"No, nothing is mixed up. Nebuchadnezzar will be king of Babylon. Just wait. When he becomes king, you will know that the rest of what I am saying is true also."

A voice from the back, one of the Sidonians, said, "Our prophets are telling us that we will have to resist an attack from the king of Babylon. But they say that if we fight with determination we will win and never have to serve the king of Babylon."

Since some of God's words described this attitude exactly, I continued my message as if I had not been interrupted:
" ' "But if any nation or kingdom will not
serve this Nebuchadnezzar king of Babylon,
and put its neck under the yoke of the king of Babylon,
I will punish that nation with the sword, with famine,
and with pestilence, declares the Lord,
until I have consumed it by his hand.
So do not listen to your prophets, your diviners,
your dreamers, your fortune-tellers, or your sorcerers,
who are saying to you,
'You shall not serve the king of Babylon.'
For it is a lie that they are prophesying to you,

---

[114] Jeremiah 27:4-7

[115] It is not known exactly when this prophecy was made, but it appears that Nebuchadnezzar became king shortly after he defeated Pharaoh Neco at the Battle of Carchemish, which gave him immediate control over Syria and Sidon. Shortly after that, he also defeated Jehoiakim in Jerusalem. As such, it is most likely that Jeremiah's prophecy of Nebuchadnezzar was made before he became king.

with the result that you will be removed
far from your land,
and I will drive you out, and you will perish.
But any nation that will bring its neck
under the yoke of the king of Babylon and serve him,
I will leave on its own land, to work it and dwell there,
declares the Lord." ' "[116]

"You say that our prophets are lying," said one of the diplomats from Tyre, "and they will say that you are lying. How can we know who to believe?"

"Yahweh's true prophets have made many prophecies in the past that have been fulfilled," I argued. "Even when Israel was originally led out of Egypt into this land, that was predicted by Yahweh beforehand. Are your gods so reliable at telling the future?"

"I think you might be being a bit selective, Jeremiah," responded Dishon, drily. "Wasn't there a prophet called Jonah who foretold that Nineveh would be destroyed in 40 days? But it didn't happen for ages."

"Yahweh is a forgiving God. When Jonah made the prophecy, Nineveh repented immediately, and Yahweh forgave. But later they went back to their old ways, so Yahweh's judgement came on them."

"A convenient explanation," said another, "but how can we be sure?"

"Watch Nebuchadnezzar," I replied. "I don't think you will have to wait long before he is king of Babylon. And don't forget to tell your kings about the yoke!"

---

[116] Jeremiah 27:8-11

Chapter 12

A cup for all

April, 605 BC – the 4th year of King Jehoiakim

By the start of the fourth year of Jehoiakim, it was clear to almost everyone that Babylon was the nation to fear.

Optimists still hoped for a miracle, and Pharaoh Neco had indeed met with some unexpected successes in the previous year. But Nebuchadnezzar had just replaced his father as the commander of Babylon's armies, and events seemed to be building up to a crescendo. Pharaoh Neco and his army had already headed north again, and the combined armies of Assyria and Egypt would soon meet that of Babylon under the newly unleashed brilliance of Nebuchadnezzar's leadership. Pharaoh was imagining victory, an Egyptian empire expanding into Assyria and beyond[117] – but the enemy had regrouped and taken a different approach. Much is uncertain in war.

---

[117] Jeremiah 46:8

On the fringes of the once-great Assyrian empire, in the areas surrounding Judah, practical leaders were forging treaties of support and cooperation, while preparing for the worst.

What frustrated me most was that none of them took the opportunity to even explore the possibility of declaring their support for Babylon before events forced it on them. Not one made the choice to place the yoke of Babylon on their neck and the necks of their people.

Once again, God's advice was ignored.

In Judah, life went on as usual, as its rulers concentrated on their own comfort and appearances. The ordinary people were to pay a high price for this irresponsible leadership. Sadly, though, they didn't really care and refused to believe it was coming.

Jehoiakim continued to reshape and beautify his palace, and exploit his people in the process. Many artisans laboured hard for the king, only to receive little or no reward for their work.[118] Workers began to do their best to avoid his notice. The palace grew outwards and upwards, its new rooms panelled with cedar and painted in brilliant red.[119]

But outside the palace, the city was being painted in the darker red of innocent blood.[120] As a youth, Jehoiakim had delighted in violence; once king, his delight had few constraints. And he was not short of helpers – oppression spread through the city and on throughout the nation, with Jehoiakim's closest supporters leading the way.

As usual, the worship of false gods contributed many more deaths. The slaughter of young, innocent children had taken root again in Topheth, pausing briefly to gather

---

[118] Jeremiah 22:13
[119] Jeremiah 22:14
[120] Jeremiah 22:17

its strength and then growing like a luxuriant weed, spreading its unmitigated cruelty across the city that should have been dedicated to Yahweh, the God of compassion and long-suffering love.

In just three years, Jehoiakim had liberated evil from the restraint placed on it by Josiah and made violence once again the language of the city.

Yet I was not a target. Despite my ongoing criticism and condemnation of evil, I remained alive and free, while many others languished in Jehoiakim's dungeons. It seemed another irresistible display of the invisible hand of God.

Since overcoming my fear during that night of suffering in the stocks, everything had become much easier. God's promise of protection had held firm and my confidence had grown again: changed in focus, but strengthened nevertheless. I no longer expected to be kept free of suffering, but I knew that I would always be able to deliver God's message whatever might happen. They would never be able to overcome me when I was delivering God's words.

And God continued to give me ever more words to deliver.

More details were provided about the coming catastrophe. Judah, God said, would become a ruin and a waste. Judah and all the surrounding nations would serve Babylon for seventy years, after which judgement – a final judgement – would in turn fall upon her.[121]

God's warnings, strident though they had already been throughout the 23 years of my prophesying, were gradually crystallising, and the details were no more pleasant than the sweeping statements had been.

---

[121] Jeremiah 25:11-12

Fiery letters still glowed on the wall of my mind each day. The urge to act immediately on any new instruction from God was still a familiar experience for me. At times, the impulse to speak took command of me and I literally could not keep silent. My mind seemed full to overflowing with words which I could not forget, but could not always order or understand.

Yet still the words kept coming.

The instruction which initiated what turned out to be one of the biggest assignments of my entire career came very early in the fourth year of Jehoiakim, before the Battle of Carchemish and the accession of King Nebuchadnezzar which followed soon after. In fact, it came before any of the significant events of that tumultuous year, events that marched one after another in quick succession and removed any vestiges of doubt that judgement had indeed begun for the house of Judah.

CR

I awoke abruptly and completely, the blackness and stillness that surrounded me as I lay in bed providing no clue as to the reason for this strange alertness. Rolling over, I strained to see in the dark and listened for any hint of what could have woken me. There was nothing to see and nothing to hear. What had caused this unusual disturbance in my sleep? I felt so unsettled by it that I sat up in bed, silent in the dark, and strained once more to hear or see anything at all. It was then that I sensed a change in the room and began to wonder whether this was the hand of God. There was no sudden change, but slowly, imperceptibly, the room gained a centre of light. The light did not seem to spread or to fill the room, but remained centred on itself, as if contained and restrained from spreading outwards. Seated on my mat, I found myself drawn into this cocoon of growing light, part of a scene that was infinitely larger than my room. Slowly the vista spread until it seemed to encompass a vast expanse of glory that was remote, yet filled with intricate detail in every area. Anything I focused on could be seen in all its exquisite perfection, but there was altogether too much to take in. I can't really describe the splendour I saw, but somehow, I knew that I was seeing Yahweh, the infinite one. Held out towards me was a cup – a plain, simple, everyday cup – filled to the brim with a frothing, foaming liquid. He spoke:

"Take from my hand this cup of the wine of wrath,
and make all the nations to whom I send you drink it.
They shall drink and stagger and be crazed
because of the sword that I am sending among them."[122]

So I reached out and took the cup from God's hand – it terrifies me now to think of doing so, but it seemed natural at the time – and as I took it, he listed the nations he wanted me to give the cup to. It was a very long list. Nations to the north, south, east and west, near and far, some even across the western sea. I held the cup as I listened, and the wine of God's wrath continued its turbulent bubbling. The list concluded with the king of Babylon himself: he would drink last.

Then God went on:

"Then you shall say to them,
'Thus says the Lord of hosts, the God of Israel:
Drink, be drunk and vomit, fall and rise no more,
because of the sword that I am sending among you.' "[123]

Maybe because my words have been rejected so often, it occurred to me to wonder whether all of the kings would so meekly accept a cup of foaming wine from the hand of an itinerant foreign prophet. God answered my thoughts:

---

[122] Jeremiah 25:15-16
[123] Jeremiah 25:27

"And if they refuse to accept the cup
from your hand to drink,
then you shall say to them,
'Thus says the Lord of hosts: You must drink!
For behold, I begin to work disaster at the city
that is called by my name, and shall you go unpunished?
You shall not go unpunished,
for I am summoning a sword against all the inhabitants
of the earth, declares the Lord of hosts.' "[124]

Armies would soon fight, and shape the history of the world by their tumult, but Yahweh announced himself as Yahweh of armies. He would oversee their ferment and guide their turmoil in his anger.

Many other words were spoken to me by Yahweh at that time. It was the most direct experience of the presence of God that I have ever had. I saw him and he spoke to me – it must have been a vision, for no man can see our God and live – but it was a lengthy personal briefing, and maybe the magnitude of the event reflected the scale and importance of the task he was setting me. All of his words were frightening in their menace, but one sentence in particular caught my attention:

"Wail, you shepherds, and cry out,
and roll in ashes, you lords of the flock,
for the days of your slaughter and dispersion have come,
and you shall fall like a choice vessel."[125]

I pictured the elegant and beautiful pot I had shattered in Topheth, its shards left strewn across the roadway to be trodden underfoot by heedless travellers – and realised that this was to be the fate of Judah's leaders and the leaders of all the nations when God's judgement would be unleashed.

---

[124] Jeremiah 25:28-29
[125] Jeremiah 25:34

And then, suddenly, the audience was over. Yahweh had finished his instructions, and all that was left was for me to carry them out.

The vision disappeared, while the light in my eyes faded more slowly. A pale light of dawn could be seen shining dimly through the cracks in the shutters as I sat on my mat and tried to collect my thoughts. How long had the vision lasted? The darkness had been absolute when I had woken, startled, but now the night was over. The usual demand for action was all that remained to prove that the indescribable hours spent in the presence of Yahweh had not been just an ephemeral dream.

೧

May, 605 BC – the 4th year of King Jehoiakim

As the morning light strengthened around me, I sat alone looking out to sea and meditating. Waves rolled endlessly towards me and a gentle breeze stirred my hair. Behind me, the sun was rising above the hill country of Judah.

Sea-birds were calling above me and the feeling of being enfolded by a restful beauty was delightful. In the month since God had commissioned me to present the cup of his wrath to so many kingdoms, I had done as much as I could. Since the threat was to come from the north, I had decided that it would be best to visit some of the northern kingdoms first – before the Chaldeans arrived. This conclusion had been strengthened by my realisation that Syria had not been included in my list of target kingdoms. For Syria, it was already too late. Within weeks, they would be feeling the yoke of Nebuchadnezzar, and no warnings could make any difference.

Before leaving Jerusalem, I had made sure that King Jehoiakim and his officials were all offered the cup of God's wrath. Not one would accept it from my hand, and all had laughed at God's statement that they must drink it. These were the very men whose leadership had guaranteed that Judah must wholly consume the wine in that most unwelcome cup, yet they refused to acknowledge it. Others who deserved it less would have to share that cup of foaming wine when it was forced on all the inhabitants of Judah and Jerusalem.[126]

My brother Azariah had heard of my interview with the king, and summoned me the next day. We had not talked for several months, but this time he was determined to tell me off for my childish behaviour in presenting the picture-parable of a cup of wine.

"It's all rather juvenile, Jeremiah," he said, determined to do what he considered to be his job as an oldest brother – and a High Priest as well!

"No," I replied, as calmly as I could, "it is deadly serious. This cup contains the wrath of our God, and his wrath will destroy both our city and our nation. Maybe nothing can be done to stop it, now, but a humble response would surely minimise the damage – as it did with Josiah."

"You have been talking about destruction for more than twenty years now, Jeremiah, and it never happens. You've lost your credibility." He pursed his lips, then laughed and continued, "Anyway, if you want to warn them against bad behaviour, giving them a cup of wine doesn't seem like a good way to do it. Haven't you heard about the parties they have in the palace? Is adding more wine going to help? You'll just make the problem worse!"

"Well, you are also an official of this nation, Azariah, so I have brought the cup here for you to drink from too." I held out the cup which I had brought.

He brushed my hand away in contemptuous refusal, saying, "Don't be silly, Jeremiah."

---

[126] Jeremiah 49:12

"You must drink," I said, following God's script.

"I won't lend any credibility to your childish follies," he replied, "and you can't make me."

" 'Thus says the Lord of hosts,' " I insisted: " 'Behold, disaster is going forth from nation to nation, and a great tempest is stirring from the farthest parts of the earth!' "

"Oh, stop the performance, Jeremiah!" Azariah responded angrily. "Just leave us alone and get on with doing something useful."

It was clear that my brother would never listen to me, so after a while, I left. One nation had been presented with the wine of God's wrath. One nation had completely refused to accept God's commands and was ignoring his words.

As soon as the Feast of Unleavened Bread was over, I had hurried off to visit Tyre and Sidon, knowing that I had little time before the Feast of Weeks would demand my return to Jerusalem.

At this time, I reaped the rewards of having visited so many nations in past years. I knew the layout of the cities I must visit, and some of the diplomats I had met before were still in positions of importance. In Sidon, I had spoken to one of the men I had met in Jerusalem the previous year. He remembered me and the yoke I had worn. And he told me that the king of Sidon was very concerned about the wars being waged to the north. The Assyrians had moved to Carchemish, which could easily be their last possible haven. The future of the entire region would depend on the strength of the two main contenders: Egypt and Babylon. No-one, he said, could predict the result.

"Ah, but Yahweh can," I said, interrupting his worried report. "Did your king listen to the message about the yoke of Babylon?"

"He listened, but he wasn't quite sure what he should do."

"So he did nothing?" I asked.

"No, he has continued to talk to other nations to find out what they plan to do – but maybe you can help us. If Yahweh is telling you what will happen, how long will it be before the danger from the north strikes?"

"I can't tell you exactly when it will be, but it won't be very long," I said carefully, then explained, "That is why I am here."

"Well, why should we obey your words when you can't give us the information we need?"

"They aren't my words," I reminded him, "they are the words of Yahweh of armies – and you will just have to trust him. He has shown his power many times through history."

"But not in recent years. The king says he can't be sure enough of Yahweh's words."

"And so he has disobeyed Yahweh's instructions. Well, now the message is more insistent than ever. I need to see the king to give him a cup to drink from – the cup of Yahweh's anger."

In the end, the king of Sidon would not drink from the cup. He needed more proof, and God was not offering any more. The proof would come with the judgement.

I had then travelled to Tyre, but the welcome there was even less positive. The king of Tyre would not listen to Yahweh. He was confident that an alliance could be put together that would repel any dangers from the north. He had also pointed out, rather smugly, that no army would be likely to attack them anyway, since they had a perfect escape route available – their heavily fortified island sitting securely just a short distance offshore.

At that point, time was running out: I had to return to Jerusalem very soon. I opened the scroll on which I had written the words of Yahweh, and reviewed the list of the kings I must see. I had already decided that I had no time to travel further north, and so I planned instead to quickly visit the cities of the Philistines: Ashkelon, Gaza, Ekron and Ashdod, before hurrying to Jerusalem for the feast.

And as I sat looking out to sea that morning, only Gaza remained to be visited. A late spring had given me as much time as possible, but still, I must be walking towards Jerusalem before the day finished. If the king of Gaza could not be warned quickly, I would have to come back later. But God was with me, and, remarkably, it was still morning when I was ushered in to see the king. As with all of the other kings, he refused the cup of wine I offered to him, although he listened seriously enough to the message that accompanied it. Most of the kings I had spoken to had found Yahweh's words *almost* convincing. Almost, but not quite. They couldn't quite bring themselves to take the necessary leap of faith.

That afternoon, I hurried out of Philistine territory and walked quickly towards Jerusalem.

Once again, God had kept me safe through the many dangers of travel, the dangers of authorities in suspicious foreign cities, and the dangers of kings made angry by the uncompromising words of Yahweh.

I entered Jerusalem with little time to spare. The Sabbath preceding the feast was about to begin.

Although I did not know it at the time, on that very day, away in the north near the Euphrates River where the king of Egypt waited in Carchemish, Nebuchadnezzar and the army of Babylon were approaching, preparing for battle.

Finally, something definite was happening! After 23 years of prophesying, my words would begin to be vindicated. Although I knew what horror and devastation it would bring to my people, it was hard not to rejoice.

ᴄʀ

The Feast of Weeks had just finished when Ahikam, the son of Shaphan, came to me in Jerusalem and asked about my latest journey to Sidon and Tyre. He wanted news.

"Pharaoh Neco is in Carchemish," I told him. "The last remnants of the Assyrian army and their king are with him, but Neco and his army are the only real power they have."

"And what about Babylon?" he asked. "Who is their king, and who is leading the army?"

"Nabopolassar is still king," I replied, "but Nebuchadnezzar is leading the army – with some support from the Medes and the Persians."

"What will happen? Has God told you?"

I answered him with all that I knew at the time: "God hasn't told me exactly when things will happen, just that judgement will come with Nebuchadnezzar."

Ahikam asked a few more questions, and then we parted. I was returning to Anathoth, so I left Jerusalem through the Benjamin Gate. As I walked alone around the hills on my way to Anathoth, God gave me more news. It came with a vision that filled my eyes and stopped me in my tracks. His words described what I was seeing in the vision:

"Prepare buckler and shield, and advance for battle!
Harness the horses; mount, O horsemen!
Take your stations with your helmets,
polish your spears, put on your armour!"[127]

---

[127] Jeremiah 46:3-4

An army, obviously Egyptian, was preparing for battle. Infantrymen were checking their equipment, horsemen readying their horses. And in the distance, another army was approaching, clad in the armour of Babylon and other eastern powers.

Quickly, the vision faded and my eyes saw again the hillsides around Anathoth. This was the first time God had ever spoken without giving me some work to do.

"Why have I seen it?"[128] I asked, but God gave no answer – at least, not immediately. What was the meaning of this vision, I wondered? Egypt and Babylon were expected to meet in battle soon. Was God telling me of a battle that had been, a battle just beginning, or a battle yet to come?

Since there seemed nothing else to do, I returned to our home in Anathoth. My mother still lived there by herself, although I stayed there too when God's work permitted. Later in the day, the vision continued. This time I saw Egyptian soldiers running away, while death and destruction pursued them. There was terror on every side. And God's words described the carnage:

"They are dismayed and have turned backward.
Their warriors are beaten down and have fled in haste;
they look not back –
terror on every side!
declares the Lord.

"The swift cannot flee away, nor the warrior escape;
in the north by the river Euphrates
they have stumbled and fallen."[129]

God showed me Pharaoh's hopes and plans: Egypt rising like the Nile to overrun the kingdoms,[130] – but

---

128 Jeremiah 46:5
129 Jeremiah 46:5-6
130 Jeremiah 46:7-9

Nebuchadnezzar, as God's servant, had put an end to such plans.

Four years before, Yahweh had used Pharaoh Neco to do his work among the nations. Now the time for Pharaoh's punishment had come, and God pronounced his judgement:

"That day is the day of the Lord God of hosts,
a day of vengeance, to avenge himself on his foes.
The sword shall devour and be sated
and drink its fill of their blood.
For the Lord God of hosts holds a sacrifice
in the north country by the river Euphrates."[131]

Egypt had fallen. From what I found out later, the battle between Neco and Nebuchadnezzar probably happened on the very day that God showed me the vision. I may even have watched scenes from the battle as it happened. Yahweh's power is unbounded.

Pharaoh Neco had killed Josiah, and I felt pleased that Egypt had suffered and fled before Nebuchadnezzar. But if Egypt could not defeat Babylon, who could? How long would it be before Judah too was filled with terror on every side?

---

[131] Jeremiah 46:10

Chapter 13

Dictation

June, 605 BC – the 4th year of King Jehoiakim

Shortly after the Feast of Weeks, it became clear that my interview with Azariah was to have consequences that I had not expected. One morning I received a visit from a temple messenger, one of the Levites, who summoned me to appear the next day in the temple before a panel of the elders of the priests to answer "certain charges". Apparently, the hearing was a revival of earlier efforts to exclude me from the priesthood.

When I had turned thirty, back in the days of Josiah, some of the priests had argued that I should not be ordained as a priest because I had left my calling to become a prophet. In the end, though, I had been accepted on the basis that there was no actual conflict between the duties of a priest and those of a prophet.

Now, my enemies had renewed their attacks on me, once again claiming that I had abandoned my position as priest, but also arguing that I was bringing the office of priest into disrepute by my behaviour.

I attended the temple the next day as ordered, but the hearing was a mere mockery. My enemies, including Pashhur and Immer, argued briefly that the position of priest should be an exclusive position and that no priest should hold any other job. Of course, Benaiah, the son of Jehoiada, one of David's mighty men and the chief of Solomon's army, had been a priest,[132] but they argued that he had ceased to work as a priest. Their main argument, however, was that what I said in my prophesying was demeaning the office of priest. They used a circular argument that Immer must have known was false, but no-one – other than me – had any interest in arguing against it.

A priest, they said, was to work in the temple and uphold its holiness in all circumstances. Thus, it was obvious, they continued, that no priest should ever reflect negatively on the holiness of God's house by saying that it would or should be destroyed. Such behaviour would be making the temple unclean, so no priest who did such a thing should be allowed to work as a priest. This was my crime by their assessment.

Originally, God had made it clear that his blessing of the temple was conditional on the obedience of his people,[133] but these priests thought that they could tie Yahweh to this house even when they were treating it as a den of robbers.

After a brief hearing, the elders decided that I was to be banned from entering the house of Yahweh.[134]

Just think about it: I, a priest of God, was forbidden from entering the house of God because I had spoken the words of God. But the elders refused to believe that the words were God's words because they did not want to hear

---

[132] 1 Chronicles 27:5-6
[133] 1 Kings 9:3-9; 2 Chronicles 7:16-22
[134] Jeremiah 36:5

them. Instead, they accused me of making the temple unholy because I had repeated God's criticisms of the people who truly were making it unholy. On that basis, they had made it impossible for God to ever criticise his people or their behaviour in his temple. For God to do this, they argued, would be making his temple unholy, and they would not accept that as a possibility. They would not permit God to judge his people. But God would judge them whether they liked it or not.

One final point hurt more than the rest of that absurd judgement: my brother Azariah – despite being the High Priest – was not at the hearing. This was a religious matter. If you like, he was boss! But not only did he make no effort to support me, it seemed most likely to me that he had instigated the entire business but was too ashamed to admit it.

Even Gemariah, my other brother, did not lift a finger to support me or to reject the absurd process that was used to find me guilty on a trumped-up charge. Instead, by his silence, he supported Azariah and Immer against me. I don't suppose that he could have done much to help, but it hurt that he didn't even try. Apparently, he too thought of me as a troublemaker who should be excluded from the house of God.

My mother could see what a travesty it was, but she couldn't do anything either. As a loyal wife, she had supported her husband for many years despite her doubts; now, as a mother, she was torn between supporting her oldest son or her youngest son. God's word can often cause difficulties in families, but in the end, his way is the only right way.

℞

As a priest without a job, I was left with nothing tying me to Judah. Since the task of carrying the cup of God's wrath to many nations was still incomplete, the next day I made plans to leave. There was no more news about the conflict in the north of Syria, so I intended to visit as many of the nations in the north as I could. I felt a little apprehensive about entering an area of conflict, but work was work, and it had to be done.

As I was getting my baggage ready that afternoon, God spoke to me with a quiet word of instruction:

> "Take a scroll and write on it all the words
> that I have spoken to you
> against Israel and Judah and all the nations,
> from the day I spoke to you,
> from the days of Josiah until today.
> It may be that the house of Judah
> will hear all the disaster that I intend to do to them,
> so that every one may turn from his evil way,
> and that I may forgive their iniquity and their sin."[135]

I remember that afternoon very clearly, so clearly that I can still picture the moving shadows and hear the soft tapping as the shutters moved in the gentle breeze. Another chance was being offered to Judah and I couldn't really believe it. God's commands about the wine of his wrath had given me confidence that finally events were moving which could not be stopped. To be honest, I had been pleased. My 23 years of prophesying and waiting for judgement to come had become very wearing and had tested my faith severely. I wanted certainty and I wanted action. The vision of the cup of God's wrath had given me that certainty, and now it seemed to be slipping through my fingers again.

Not only that, but writing down all of the messages from 23 years of frequent communication with God was no small task! Words against Judah and Israel and words against every nation around had filled my head, and none

---

[135] Jeremiah 36:2-3

of them had yet been properly fulfilled. And now, it seemed most likely that their fulfilment would be delayed again until I had done this next task and my nation had once more rejected God's offer of forgiveness. I was fairly confident that they would do so, but why give them another chance? They had just expelled me from the temple for reporting God's threats, and now they were being given yet another chance. How many chances had God already given them? I was not the first prophet to speak against their unfaithfulness, God had been sending messengers for hundreds of years.

How long would I have to wait for God's promised destruction to come? I remember wondering briefly whether it would *ever* really happen; maybe some other prophet would suddenly appear and speak to King Jehoiakim as Jonah had to the king of Nineveh, and convince them all! I was confident that if things followed that path, God would forgive, and I would be left looking a fool as all of my prophecies turned to dust.

Even after 23 years of working for God, I still had much to learn. God is patient and continues to offer people more chances. When God promises destruction, he still always seems ready – even eager – to withdraw the promise if only people will repent. And it is God himself, not me, who is laying himself open to being ignored because he doesn't punish quickly enough.

I can imagine a world where God puts an angel behind each person with a sword of judgement to be used when first they sin. But it would be a world with no people, for all have sinned.

I can also imagine a world where God puts an angel behind each person to give a word of warning whenever they lean towards sin. But God wants us to choose his way based on what we know of him, not through ceaseless warning.

These things I can see now, but on that afternoon, all I could see was that I, Jeremiah, was not happy with God opening the door for my people – yet again. It seemed to me that if God opened the door for them, he was closing it for me, and it seemed completely unf… But, no, I couldn't bring myself to say that, even in my mind.

I stopped packing, stopped planning – even stopped feeling that I had a purpose.

That evening, I spoke to my mother. I don't want to get carried away with philosophy, but sometimes it really strikes me that if we had to walk God's way completely on our own, we wouldn't have a chance. We really do need others, and even when it seems as though we are completely alone, it is never quite true. I have often felt completely alone, but in fact, God has always provided people to give help when I've really needed it.

This time, my mother talked me through my problems and frustrations, and helped me to convince myself that God's fairness was never in question, unless it was that he was too generous to all of us.

So, the next day I collected together all of the scrolls on which I had written the words of God. From the very start, I had written down most of God's words on small scrolls as I received them. If I just wrote out the few messages from God that I had not already written down, I would have a full set of scrolls. Of course, there would be no difficulty in writing out these remaining messages because they were all written indelibly in my memory, still glowing every day on what I call the wall of my mind.

But a collection of scrolls was probably not what God wanted. God had commanded "a scroll." Just one. Not only that, but my writing was so untidy that many people would not be able to read the scrolls anyway.

What should I do?

Given that I was 40 years old at the time, I did not believe that I would be able to suddenly improve the legibility of my writing, so instead I started to think who I might be able to get to write out a new, neat copy of God's words.

My father's handwriting had also been poor, so he had always used scribes to write for him when it was necessary to present a document well. One such scribe had been an old man called Maaseiah. He had died shortly after my father, but he had had a grandson called Baruch, who was also a scribe and whom I knew slightly. Baruch was in his mid-twenties at the time and was already known as a reliable and accurate scribe, probably one of the best, and quite ambitious, so I approached him about the task.

Once I had described the task – and given him samples of my writing to make sure that he could decipher it – he agreed for what I considered quite a reasonable rate, given his expertise. For various reasons, I no longer had as much money as the family had had throughout my childhood. Not only that, but I no longer had any access to the tithes and offerings that God had provided for his priests. Since I could not enter the temple for "disciplinary reasons", the food had been refused me by the temple hierarchy. This was one way of trying to bring me under the control of the priests, particularly my brother Azariah, but it was not going to work. Nevertheless, the fact remained that I was no longer able to spend money as freely as I had all my life. It had already been a learning experience for me, and was to become even more difficult as time went on.

Baruch and I had agreed that I would dictate to him the messages from God which I had not already written down. These would not be in order like the rest of the scrolls, since they came from various different times during my career. You may ask why I had written down some of

God's words and not others, and the answer is really just stubbornness. Some of God's words I had found too hard, or too blunt. If you wanted to paint it in a bad light, you could say that I had been censoring God's words, and you would probably be right. But now they would all be written down.

Baruch wrote each missing section down at my dictation, with notes as to when each had occurred so that they could be fitted into the right places chronologically with the other scrolls.

Since I could not afford to pay for Baruch to spend all of his time on this scroll, he would only be spending about one third of his time on my assignment.

For me, my main goal was to set up Baruch so that he could do the work without needing me there. This would leave me free to continue my plan of carrying the cup of God's wrath to the nations of the north.

So it was that, after finishing a few days of dictation, I left Jerusalem again, heading north.

☙

Although I am trying to make this diary retell my work in order, I think it is worth tidying up this little section here.

As Baruch worked his way patiently through the words of Yahweh, writing them in his beautifully artistic script, he found the threats of destruction and death rather overpowering. He started to lose sleep and his health began to suffer. If only God's words had had that effect on more people! But he told me of his difficulties when I returned at different times, and God gave him words of comfort which guaranteed him his life despite the destruction that would go on around him.

However, there was one catch to the comfort that God freely offered him. Baruch was an ambitious man and

Yahweh told him bluntly:

> "And do you seek great things for yourself?
> Seek them not, for behold,
> I am bringing disaster upon all flesh,
> declares the Lord."[136]

Baruch found this restriction hard to accept, as many others have done before him, but he found the other prophecies of Yahweh so convincing that he accepted this demand as well. Sometimes, the times in which we live make an ordinary career impossible.

If only Ahikam, the son of Shaphan, could have made the same concession to the plans of Yahweh.

---

[136] Jeremiah 45:5

Chapter 14

They are coming!

July, 605 BC – the 4th year of King Jehoiakim

"Welcome," said Shobai, and his warm smile showed that the welcome was genuine. He stepped forward and greeted me, saying, "The Lord bless you, Jeremiah, it is wonderful to see you again. Come inside."

He stepped aside and waved me into the house, saying, "I'll just tell Maacah and Mishael that you are here. You must stay and share our evening meal. Maacah's cooking continues to improve, you know." He laughed and continued, "Yes, even though she was already peerless, she still gets better. Mishael and I are spoiled beyond words."

We entered the house and Shobai shut the door behind us. Darkness was falling, just as it had been on my first visit to Bethel, on the day, more than twenty years before, when I had first met Shobai. This time, I had chosen my time carefully to make sure that Shobai would be home from his work as a trader. His hard work over the years had been rewarded by the development of a successful wholesale business, and he now had many men working for him, buying produce from the local farmers and delivering it to traders who sold it in the markets of Bethel and the surrounding towns. But despite his success, he and Maacah had continued to live in the house he had inherited from his parents, instead of moving to the richer parts of the town.

As we passed into the main room of the house, Shobai called, "Maacah, Jeremiah has come to share our evening meal."

Across the room, Shobai's fourteen-year-old son sat at a table. He had put down his pen as we entered and now he stood and came quickly over to greet me. "My lord Jeremiah, welcome," he said in a voice that was – most of the time – much deeper than when I had last met him. The voice was a pleasant mix of his father's and his mother's voices, and sounded warm and welcoming.

"How are your studies going, Mishael?" I asked.

"I am enjoying them," he answered. "We learn a lot of history, and lots about world events and other kingdoms. We study many religious themes too – some good, but most bad."

As he spoke, Maacah came into the room and she too greeted me warmly. She was still slim – an unusual attribute in one who could cook as well as she did – her dark hair was still long and flowing, and her smile was still entrancing.

I greeted her as briefly as I could without being rude, then looked away again to ask Mishael, "What are you writing at the moment?" There were two opened scrolls lying on the bench, one of which was mostly empty, so it was obvious that he was copying a scroll.

"You may be surprised, but I am copying the Book of the Law of Yahweh," said the young man. "My father wants me to balance the bad religious ideas that I get taught with the good ones from our God. So it's not really part of my studies, but it does help."

I walked over to the bench and examined his new scroll. "Your writing is very neat," I commented, rather impressed by the clear and mature handwriting that was filling the scroll. "You could almost be a scribe already. Your writing is much better than mine. At the moment, I am paying a scribe in Jerusalem to copy out God's prophecies. If I had your skill, I wouldn't need to."

Shobai said proudly, "Mishael is the best writer in his class, and probably the best student in all Bethel."

Mishael looked embarrassed and tried to change the subject: "The Book of the Law of God is a wonderful expression of how God wants us to live, isn't it?"

The conversation continued, and after a while, Maacah left the room, saying that she must go and make sure that there would be enough food for everyone, since her mother, Miriam, would also be joining them soon.

Mishael was Shobai and Maacah's only surviving child. Two other sons had been born after him, but both had died in early childhood.

Miriam arrived just a short time later and greeted me with wheezing happiness. She was still an enthusiastic follower of Yahweh, but was slowing down a little with age. There had always been a good relationship between her and Mishael, and they were each obviously pleased to see the other. Apparently, he planned to make a copy of the Book of the Law for Miriam too, once he had practised by making a copy for himself. Unfortunately, as events worked out, he was never able to complete the task.

As old friends, we quickly fell back into the easy companionship and conversation we had developed over the years. The only awkwardness was on my part because of Maacah, and I always did my best to hide that. The whole family was still dedicated to God in a way that was very encouraging to me after my recent experiences in Jerusalem.

During dinner, the latest news was discussed. Just that day, news had arrived of a battle at Carchemish between Babylon and Egypt. Nebuchadnezzar's army had defeated the army of Pharaoh Neco, more than twice its own size, through exquisitely clever tactics.

"I'm sure Nebuchadnezzar is a good tactician," I remarked, as Shobai reported this news, "but he would have won even if he had been blind and all his army sick. God is fulfilling his prophecies, so the result was never in doubt."

"So what will happen next?" asked Shobai. "We are told that Nebuchadnezzar has completely destroyed the remnants of the Assyrian army, and has overrun Syria with very little resistance from anyone. People here are frightened that he might be coming here soon."

"It's an unpleasant idea, but I'm afraid that you will have to accept it," I responded. "Nebuchadnezzar is going to continue to move south, and soon Judah will be his target."

I had explained the reasons for my visit earlier, and now Miriam asked, "But, Jeremiah, if Nebuchadnezzar goes to those areas straight away, how will you warn all of the northern nations about his coming before he gets there? And it will be very dangerous to move around in the north, won't it?"

I had to admit that I hadn't thought about it that way, although it should have been very obvious.

"Maybe I won't be able to visit the northern kingdoms now," I mused.

"But Yahweh wouldn't tell you to do that work if there was no time to do it in, would he?" she persisted.

Her comments made sense, and they made even more sense as events unfolded, but for the time being I only knew that I had a job to do, and must do my best to complete it.

We shared a delightful meal, and the fellowship was equally special. This family was full of the joy of God's ways, even though they were almost alone in Bethel now. Over the years, the others with whom they had shared the worship of Yahweh had either moved away to other towns or been distracted by the returning worship of idols. Once Josiah's influence had dissipated, Bethel's worship had begun to decline as Judah's continued to do. Shobai and his family were now the only ones from Bethel who travelled to Jerusalem for the feasts each year, and even they had found it hard to be consistent in the face of both apathy and opposition.

Miriam's inn still attracted many visitors, and the visitors didn't stop coming at feast times. Since Maacah's marriage, Miriam had gone back to doing the cooking for the inn, and had found a helper, a stern, spare woman, to look after the customers.

Miriam looked at me with a laughing smile and said, "You know how I always complained that the stairs kept getting steeper and steeper? Well, now my helper does all of the work upstairs, so I haven't been upstairs at all for the last year or so."

Apparently this helper could manage the inn completely if Miriam was away, using fill-in cooks to supply the evening meal, but it wasn't the same; the visitors said that they preferred Miriam's cooking, and her hearty welcome too. I could understand why.

After the meal was finished, Shobai and Miriam asked me to find an interesting section of the Book of the Law and talk to them about it, so we looked at the blessings and curses that God had detailed near the end of the book. It was rather a serious subject, but I wanted them to see why Nebuchadnezzar was coming and what could be expected. Mishael and Maacah were the most affected by the details of the curses and the horrific destruction that Nebuchadnezzar would be bringing. Each felt that the punishment was warranted, but feared the breadth of the suffering and the numbers of people who would suffer.

When I left Bethel the next day, I left a town in which fear was spreading. There was fear in Shobai's home also, but it was a fear for others, because they were convinced that God's words would come true.

CR

As I continued north from Bethel, I journeyed towards the coast and travelled on through Tyre and Sidon into Lebanon. It was my intention to avoid Nebuchadnezzar's forces, and to deliver God's warning of coming anger and the impending attack from Babylon to Lebanon and the other nations even further north. Predicting what will happen in international events is never easy, but after a lot of thought it seemed to me that Nebuchadnezzar was likely to attack Lebanon and those other areas very soon, probably before attacking Israel and Judah.

But even as I travelled north, an event happened that changed the entire appearance of the future: Nabopolassar, Nebuchadnezzar's father, died.

Immediately, Nebuchadnezzar returned to Babylon to claim his position as king over the empire. In his absence, the Chaldean army came to a halt. I was free to travel around and warn the kings of the smaller nations and city states of what would happen now that Nebuchadnezzar was king, and recent events had made my message even more credible. At the Battle of Carchemish, Pharaoh Neco's hopes for world domination had proved false, and now the victor was not just a successful leader, but a conquering king.

Nebuchadnezzar was a man to fear.

I spoke to kings and gave them the cup of God's wrath. No-one was laughing anymore.

Then one day, God recalled me to Jerusalem. In a voice of fiery urgency, I was told:

"Declare in Judah, and proclaim in Jerusalem, and say,
'Blow the trumpet through the land; cry aloud and say,
"Assemble, and let us go into the fortified cities!"
Raise a standard toward Zion, flee for safety, stay not,
for I bring disaster from the north, and great destruction.
A lion has gone up from his thicket,
a destroyer of nations has set out;
he has gone out from his place
to make your land a waste;
your cities will be ruins without inhabitant.
For this put on sackcloth, lament and wail,
for the fierce anger of the Lord
has not turned back from us.' "[137]

Nebuchadnezzar must have been successful in getting himself crowned king, I thought. Not only that, but he must now be sure enough of his position to be willing to leave Babylon in search of conquests. He must be confident that his people were behind him and that his army would have full support from home. A lion was truly coming; a destroyer of nations had set out.

And I must return to Judah straight away.

That night my sleep was filled with terror. I heard the alarm and the sound of war. The trumpet blew endlessly and my heart was beating wildly. Crash followed hard on crash; the whole land was laid waste. Suddenly tents were

---

[137] Jeremiah 4:5-8

laid waste, curtains torn down in a moment. I saw the battle standard unfurled and heard the urgent sound of the trumpet.[138]

I looked on the earth, and behold, it was without form and void; and to the heavens, and they had no light. I looked on the mountains, and behold, they were quaking, and all the hills moved to and fro. I looked, and behold, there was no man, and all the birds of the air had fled. I looked, and behold, the fruitful land was a desert, and all its cities were laid in ruins before the Lord, before his fierce anger.[139]

Very early the next morning, I departed, hurrying back to Judah to deliver God's words to my people once again.

As I passed through Judah, I visited many towns, shouting out the message that attackers were coming and that they should go to fortified towns. They must find places of safety.

Already, there had been attacks in the north by Syrian soldiers escaping from the Chaldean army overrunning Syria. People had heard reports of frightening things, and those who lived in the country were finally beginning to believe God's warnings.

Shortly afterwards, I arrived in Jerusalem, and immediately began proclaiming the latest warnings to all who would listen.

One piece of good news greeted me: the elders of the priests had reviewed my case and relented. No longer was I banned from entering God's temple. This was to be important in the next assignment that God had for me, so I assume that their change of heart was at Yahweh's instigation.

---

[138] Jeremiah 4:19-21
[139] Jeremiah 4:23-26

❧

One by one, they walked into the room while I held the door open for them. I had invited them all to come to this particular chamber in the temple of Yahweh and they had all come – but not without some hesitation. I was known for causing trouble and none of the family elders had appeared to welcome the invitation.

It was Jaazaniah, the leader of the family, who had received me, sitting in his tent in a crowded courtyard in the western extension of the city. I had called his name, and he had hurried out to see who was calling him.

In the last month, the city had become crowded with people fleeing the attacks of both Syrian and Chaldean raiding parties. And now Nebuchadnezzar's army had attacked the land and a siege was expected any day.

"I'm Jeremiah, the son of Hilkiah," I announced. "Are you Jaazaniah, the son of Jeremiah?"

"Yes, that is my name," Jaazaniah replied, and waited.

"I am here to invite you and your family to come to the temple of God about an important matter."

"My family?" repeated Jaazaniah, slowly. "There are many in my family. Who do you mean?"

I smiled and waved my arms to encompass the collection of tents in the courtyard. "Any of your adult male relatives who live in these tents. The whole house of the Rechabites."[140]

"I see," said Jaazaniah noncommittally.

---

[140] Jeremiah 35:3 lists only men and does not make it clear whether women and children were included in the expression "and the whole house of the Rechabites". Taken in conjunction with Jeremiah 35:8 and the indication that this was only a chamber in the temple, it appears more likely that it would only have been men – or there would have been too many people to fit in the space available.

"Can you come now?" I asked, persisting.

"Not right now," said Jaazaniah. "Some of my brothers are not here at present."

"Alright," I said, "I can come back tomorrow afternoon at about the same time. Can you make sure that everyone will be here then?"

"I suppose I can, if you really want us to come," he said doubtfully.

"I do," I confirmed.

The conversation had ended there and I had left.

On the next afternoon, a nervous-looking group of men had been waiting in their tents when I arrived. Several had asked me what it was all about, but I had answered every question with the advice that they should wait until they were all in the temple, because I had something special for them there. They had looked at each other doubtfully, but had finally followed me tentatively all the way to the temple, up the stairs and along a passageway to the door of the chamber of the sons of Hanan.

I had opened the door and then stood waiting as they filed into the room. "Each of you find a place to sit," I encouraged them, and they did so, sitting down on the seats that lined the walls of the chamber. An empty table sat in the middle of the room.

As soon as everyone was seated, I said, "I'll be back soon," and left them waiting.

It didn't take me long to fetch the large tray I had organised for the purpose. It was heavy because it held many cups, as well as two large jugs. I placed the heavily-laden tray on the table thankfully, and began to distribute the cups. The men exchanged glances, looking rather troubled, but I smiled encouragingly as I gave each man his cup.

Once the distribution was complete, I picked up one of the jugs and walked deliberately towards Jaazaniah. Every eye in the room was fixed worriedly on that jug. No-one could tell what was inside, but Jaazaniah put his hand over his cup as I approached. He looked uncertain and uncomfortable – but also determined.

"Drink wine!" I said enthusiastically, holding up the pitcher. Most of the men gasped, and nobody seemed to breathe as we all waited to see what Jaazaniah would do.

"No, we can't," said Jaazaniah, firmly.

"But why not?" I asked.

"We will drink no wine," answered Jaazaniah, "for Jonadab the son of Rechab, our father, commanded us, 'You shall not drink wine, neither you nor your sons forever. You shall not build a house; you shall not sow seed; you shall not plant or have a vineyard; but you shall live in tents all your days, that you may live many days in the land where you sojourn.' "[141]

I stood and listened, still holding the pitcher of wine.

The next oldest brother continued earnestly: "We have obeyed the voice of Jonadab the son of Rechab, our father, in all that he commanded us, to drink no wine all our days, ourselves, our wives, our sons, or our daughters, and not to build houses to dwell in. We have no vineyard or field or seed, but we have lived in tents and have obeyed and done all that Jonadab our father commanded us."[142]

"Then what has brought you to Jerusalem?" I asked, interrupting.

"When Nebuchadnezzar king of Babylon came up against the land, we said, 'Come, and let us go to Jerusalem for fear of the army of the Chaldeans and the

---

[141] Jeremiah 35:6-7
[142] Jeremiah 35:8-10

army of the Syrians.' So we are living in Jerusalem," explained Jaazaniah.

"I understand," I said, but then, suddenly, the voice of God spoke within me, explaining why he had commanded the entire sequence of events. When he finished, I noticed that the men were all watching me as if I had been behaving unusually, so I decided to answer their unspoken questions.

"God has told me to go and speak to the people of Judah and Jerusalem," I explained, "using you Rechabites as an example. God is pleased that you have obeyed your ancestor Jonadab, but disgusted that his people will not treat him with the same respect – although he has spoken to them again and again through many prophets."

"You mean that we don't have to drink this wine?" asked Jaazaniah, thankfully.

"No," I said, and couldn't help smiling again at their relieved expressions. "God was just using the wine to demonstrate your faithfulness to the commands of your forefather. Thus says the Lord of hosts, the God of Israel: 'Because you have obeyed the command of Jonadab your father and kept all his precepts and done all that he commanded you, therefore thus says the Lord of hosts, the God of Israel: Jonadab the son of Rechab shall never lack a man to stand before me.' "[143]

---

[143] Jeremiah 35:18-19

Chapter 15

Attack

When the invasion came, it came swiftly. Nebuchadnezzar had rejoined his army, but now as king and full of confidence.

They moved south with speed and brutality. There was little resistance because of the fear that went before them. Assyria had been famous for her irresistible power and merciless cruelty, but Babylon had bested her in both. I had grown up hearing of Assyria's behaviour, but God's words had described Babylon as being without mercy, eager to kill.

The next few months were to show the descendants of Jacob what it really meant to reject God's way. Nebuchadnezzar showed them that it is much better to serve God than to serve man.

A token resistance had been displayed in the north of Israel, with local militias trying briefly to defend walled towns in the hope that Nebuchadnezzar would ignore them and move on to easier targets. He didn't. Burning ruins marked his progress until other towns and cities learned the lesson. Farms and villages suffered also, and the smoke of fields and fruit trees left grey smudges on the skyline, warning all who would pay attention that their doom was coming. Refugees moved quickly, trying to stay ahead of the ravaging hordes, hoping that somewhere the destruction would stop. For those who were too slow, owners and servants alike, death or slavery were often the only choices.

King Jehoiakim heard the news in his wood-panelled palace and wondered what he should do. He knew that if he mounted a full resistance, it would be a fight to the death. Babylon had already defeated both Assyria and Egypt, so what chance did little Judah have?

Assyria had invaded Judah in the time of his great-great-grandfather Hezekiah, but Hezekiah's resistance had finally been built on faith, after his attempts to buy off the attacker had failed. King Jehoiakim had neither faith nor money, so he must muddle through without them in deep uncertainty.

Once again, I was not in Jerusalem when these events were taking place. I had travelled south to warn the kings of Ammon, Moab, Edom and the many small kingdoms in Arabia. The cup of God's wrath was coming quickly, and the nations who were to drink it must be warned or I would be failing in my duty. I spent about three months on the roads between kingdoms, and by the time I returned, it was all over. King Nebuchadnezzar had come and gone, and many captive Israelites had gone with him.

His army had surrounded Jerusalem and entered the city after a short siege and a sudden surrender, killing, maiming and mutilating.

Nebuchadnezzar entered the city intent on making a point. Jerusalem had offered resistance instead of submission, and she must be taught a lesson.

Just inside the gate, it began. Anyone who was armed or had clearly been resisting the Chaldeans was killed immediately. From there, the army spread slowly through the city, making sure that there was no resistance and looking for excuses to kill. Trying to keep gold or silver from the soldiers gave them the excuse they were looking for.

ℭℛ

The prophetess Huldah was old by that time and had become increasingly frail since the death of Josiah, and the death of Shallum her husband shortly afterward.

She heard the shouts and screams of the populace as the Chaldean soldiers worked their way through street after street, gradually coming closer. By that time, Huldah was too weak to get up and investigate, but her neighbour, Deborah, came in and explained in shrill terror what was happening. God's prophecies had warned of the coming horror for many years and Huldah knew what was to come. For her, this was a confirmation of all that she had worked for as a prophetess, so she did not share the terror felt by those around her. If anything, she felt a greater peace and confidence because God was in control and keeping his word. It was a restful feeling, despite the uncertainty about what would happen next.

Huldah was trying to calm her neighbour when suddenly a Chaldean soldier burst into the room with his sword at the ready. Deborah screamed and fainted, collapsing on the floor at the soldier's feet.

"Welcome, sir," said Huldah, calmly. "Are you a soldier of Nebuchadnezzar the king of Babylon? Yahweh my God has warned for many years that you were coming."

"Me?" asked the soldier, surprised.

"Not you particularly, young man," said Huldah with a gentle smile, "but your king and his army. Yahweh has sent you as his servants to punish Judah for her idolatry and evil. We have been waiting for many years since he first said that you would come."

"Are you an Israelite?" asked the soldier suspiciously.

"Yes."

"Then why are you welcoming an enemy? Are you a traitor?"

"I am no traitor – I am faithful to Yahweh, the God of Israel, and these are his plans you are fulfilling," she replied, her voice sounding weaker.

"Do you have any gold?" asked the soldier, tired of the discussion and wanting to get back to business.

"No, I have no gold, and it would be no use to me anyway since I am about to die. But I have seen the work of Yahweh, the fulfilment of his prophecies, and I will die in peace. If I had any gold you would be welcome to it, but gold will never help you to please Yahweh, and that is the only thing that really matters."

"I will leave you in peace, old woman, but are you sure you have no gold?"

"I have none at all," Huldah responded, and her voice sounded feeble as she continued. "There is a little silver in the pot on the shelf over there, though, and I will have no further need of it. You may take it if you want to."

The soldier looked at her in amazement, unable to understand why anyone would offer their money to a foreigner, let alone a threatening soldier!

He took one more look around the room and then turned and walked out, ignoring the silver Huldah had offered. Huldah heard the door close and looked up at the ceiling, feeling very tired.

"Has he gone?" It was the whispering voice of her neighbour who had fainted when the soldier had entered and was now lifting her head slowly from the floor.

"Yes, Deborah," said Huldah, laughing weakly. "He has gone and we are both safe." Her hand moved slowly to her forehead. "I had forgotten that you were there, with your silly fainting."

"I think that I woke up almost as soon as I fell, but I was scared to move in case he decided to attack me." Deborah sat up and then slowly stood. She looked down at Huldah, "I listened to everything you said. Why did you offer him your silver, Huldah?"

"I won't need it any more, Deborah," said Huldah gently. "I'm dying."

"It's those terrible Chaldeans," cried Deborah. "They have scared you to death."

"No, Deborah. I am at peace and content. I am sad to see the punishment of Judah, but glad to see that God still fulfils his promises." She paused and reached out her hand to Deborah. "Things will still get worse for a while, but this time will pass and Judah will be regathered."

"Can we do anything to avoid the suffering?"

"No. If everyone repented, I'm sure God would relent, but individuals will not be able to change his plans now." Once again, her voice was fading, and Deborah had to bend forward to hear her next words: "We deserve to drink the wine of his wrath and we must drink it, as Jeremiah the son of Hilkiah has told us."

"You must rest now," said Deborah, smoothing Huldah's hair with her hand. "We can talk more later."

"There will be no *later*, Deborah," whispered Huldah. "Yahweh is about to take away my breath. I will sleep in peace."

Deborah held her hand and sat in silence for a few minutes as Huldah seemed to go to sleep.

Huldah stirred once more and roused herself. "Tell Jeremiah the prophet that I am happy to have worked for our blessed creator as he has. Tell him that he needs to keep doing the good work of Yahweh and never give up. And tell him 'Peace'." There was another long pause and Deborah wondered whether her breathing had stopped. But there were two last words to be whispered slowly before she breathed no more: "Shalom, Deborah."

By the time I returned to Jerusalem faithful Huldah was long buried, but Deborah found me and recounted to me in detail the events of that day. Huldah's life had ended with the comfort and peace that only faith can bring, in the midst of the terror that spread through the city as greed and the sword claimed so many victims. Her encouraging message has been a great help to me in many times of trouble since.

☙

Elsewhere in the city, many were beaten, wounded and killed. Even more had their savings taken away by Chaldean soldiers. Indeed, it was often the gold that caused the beatings or death. Soldiers burst into homes and demanded gold. When people denied having any gold – as most did – the soldiers began to look around to see what they could find. Obviously they had had practice before, as they looked in a few common places and watched the inhabitants closely to observe when they looked the most uncomfortable.

When gold was discovered in hidden places, quite a few people foolishly tried to stop the soldiers from taking it. This often led to disaster for them: the soldiers did not carry swords for nothing. If people had taken the time to think, they would probably have responded differently, but instead, many were left wounded, dying or dead, and the gold was taken anyway. Is gold really more important than life? For Immer it was.

Immer was a very old man by that time, and quite rich, as most of the senior priests were. When two soldiers pushed open the door of his palatial house, he was lying on his bed, nibbling some dried fruit that was being passed to him by a servant. Both soldiers had their swords ready, and first looked around to see whether there was any threat to their safety. But Immer was alone except for his young manservant.

"Give me your gold," demanded the older soldier, who led the way.

"I have none here with me right now," temporised Immer.

"Oh, come on!" replied the soldier in a sneering voice. "Marble columns, timber panelling and polished stone floors, and you try to tell me you are poor. Why are all you rich like that?"

"No, no, no," said Immer, in an obsequious voice nothing like the supercilious tones he normally used when talking to his inferiors. "I do have some gold, but not here. My gold is concealed on my farm in the north of Israel, hidden in a secret cave." It was a lie, but Immer hoped that it would sound confiding enough to be believable. He rose slowly from his bed to stand before the soldier, bent over with age though he was.

"I don't believe you," stated the soldier flatly. "Maybe I should cut off your hand to help you remember where your gold is. You would still have one hand to be able to show me with." He moved threateningly, reaching out to grab Immer's wrist.

"Oh, no, sir, please," stammered Immer in terror.

"Well, where is the gold?" repeated the soldier, mercilessly, as he took hold of Immer's wrist.

"I only have a little in another room," he quavered.

"Ah," said the soldier sardonically, "so this is the 'No gold here' that you claimed, is it?" He dropped Immer's wrist in disgust.

"You must understand that I am an old man, sir," said Immer, trembling.

"Yes, an old man who tells lies," answered the soldier grimly. "An old man who deserves to die for his lies."

"Oh, no, sir, please," repeated Immer. "I will show you all the gold I have. Come into the back room and I will show you where it is hidden."

He led the way slowly into a room at the back of his house, signalling to the servant not to follow.

"Ho-ho, no sir! You come with us," said the leader of the soldiers to the servant. "We don't want you going out and finding help while we're busy with the gold."

So Immer and his servant entered the room, followed by the soldiers. Once they were in the room, Immer asked the soldier to shut the door.

"Why would I do that, old man?" asked the soldier. "You are afraid to have anyone see that you have gold here, aren't you? That makes me think that you are planning to trick me and only give me a small part of it. Have a care, old man." He gestured meaningfully with the sword which he still held in his hand.

"No, no… of course not," fluttered Immer, looking at the sword and trembling.

"Then where is the gold? Hurry."

Immer moved to the back of the room where a decorated linen wall hanging obscured the wall. He pushed the hanging aside, revealing a section of wall in which could be seen, under close inspection, a stone with no mortar around it. Immer pushed one end of the stone inward and the other end moved outward a little.

Grasping the protruding end carefully, he slowly worked it out of the wall, revealing a small space behind holding several bags tied at the neck. Immer stepped back and gestured with his hand.

The soldiers looked delighted. This was the bonus they had been hoping for. Soldiers are never paid well, their leaders always relying on the spoils of war to cover the deficit.

The older one reached into the niche with his left hand and lifted out several bags, which he put on a table at the side of the room. His younger partner put down his sword on the table and swiftly started untying the knots that held one of the bags closed. Soon bag after bag had been opened and gold coins from various lands were tipped eagerly out onto the table.

Immer looked on, still trembling with fright, but also watching worriedly. The young soldier repacked the bags and tied them up again before putting them all into a bag that he carried on his back. As he did so, the leader looked back into the secret nook, feeling around with his hand to make sure that he had not missed anything valuable.

Still holding his sword in his right hand, he scrutinised the niche again carefully, and Immer looked even more concerned. The soldier felt around again, as if something had attracted his attention. Then he seemed to be moving one of the bricks that lined the niche. After a few seconds, he pulled it out through the opening and dropped it on the floor. He reached inside again, but as he did so, Immer lunged for the sword which the younger soldier had put down on the table. He probably hoped to kill the younger soldier and then see what he could achieve after that, but he never had a chance. His fear made him miss the sword hilt and lurch to one side as he lost his balance. The young soldier shouted, even as his superior turned, holding more bags of valuables that had been hidden within an inner recess.

The leader asked no questions and wasted no time. A quick step forward and the sword in his right hand was thrust deep into Immer's side, even as he tried to regain his balance. Immer's sudden scream faded into a gurgle as he fell to the ground. The soldier quickly pulled out his sword and turned to the servant, but he had not moved and showed no signs of wanting to help his master. A master like Immer would not be missed by his servants.

As the younger soldier picked up his sword again, the leader warned Immer's servant not to give any trouble, adding, "Your master won't need your help any more now. Did he ever share any of his gold with you?"

He then noticed the bags that he was still holding in his left hand, and said to his young partner, "More treasure, hidden within an inner compartment. I guess these ones must be worth even more than the others. The old man couldn't bear to lose them, so he lost his life instead."

The two soldiers emptied the nook completely and carefully put all of the bags of valuables into the younger soldier's large bag, completely filling it.

As the two soldiers took their spoil and left, Immer lay on the floor dying. His servant tried to make him comfortable, but the old man was filled with pain and terrified at the prospect of imminent death.

The soldier's sword had done its work all too well, and the old man's life slipped away just a few minutes later. His servant straightened out the body, then went to find Immer's son, Pashhur, and pass on the news of Immer's death and the loss of his valuables.

The servant, whose name was Ishi, came to find me when I returned to Jerusalem. He told me of the circumstances of Immer's death as I have reported them here, and he also told me Immer's last words. Speaking slowly, and in great pain, he said: "Now Jeremiah will gloat over me… even in death."

Immer and Huldah, two people who had contributed to my direction in life, were both dead – but in such different ways. Huldah died in peace because she knew that her God was in control, while Immer died in terror, unable to let go of his money. God had promised terror on every side, and Immer, who had never believed God's prophecies through me, had felt it come true.

Chapter 16

Who stays, who goes?

When one nation is defeated by another nation, many things are unpredictable. When the victor is not merely a nation but a large and powerful empire whose centre is more than a thousand kilometres away, the uncertainty is even greater.

The victor has taken control of the vanquished country, and for the time being, what the victor says, goes. But can control be maintained once the army packs up its tents and departs?

Nebuchadnezzar's army had entered Jerusalem and shown its strength. Resistance had been met with crushing punishment, and large quantities of gold and precious objects had been collected to satisfy the plunderers.

Soldiers had entered Yahweh's temple and taken some of its vessels, though not too many, since Nebuchadnezzar's goal was cooperation. He did not intend to crush Judah. What he wanted was a tactical strike, powerful enough to put fear into the hearts of the people, but not destructive enough that the kingdom could no longer defend itself from the surrounding nations. If Judah was too weak, other nations would come in to fill the vacuum, and Nebuchadnezzar would be back at square one.

Ideally, such an invasion would leave the nation too afraid of Babylon to rebel, but still strong enough to instil fear in the smaller nations around it. Egypt was a problem, but Nebuchadnezzar planned to deal with that problem very soon.

King Jehoiakim was Egypt's vassal, so Nebuchadnezzar's initial plan had been to replace him with another Israelite king. However, enquiries showed that there was no real talent to choose from – or at least no-one on whom he felt he could rely.

At one stage, King Jehoiakim was even put in chains ready to be transported to Babylon,[144] but apparently he awoke to the seriousness of his situation and acted with abject humility. He promised to serve King Nebuchadnezzar faithfully, and his obsequious submissiveness won him a reprieve.

So, King Jehoiakim stayed, keeping his job because he wasn't too good at it and there didn't seem to be anyone who would be a suitable replacement.

However, there were others whom Nebuchadnezzar did not want to leave in their positions, and these he took away with him. As far as I could tell from the reports I heard, he picked out all the people who he thought would be most likely to cause trouble and took them away into captivity: nobles, princes, leaders, the intelligentsia and anyone capable of organising others. After all, an army with no leadership is only dangerous to its own people.

---

[144] 2 Chronicles 36:6

Most of the men who had been in leadership positions under Jehoiakim were considered a threat and were taken away, but apparently religious leaders were not, so my brother Azariah retained his position as High Priest.

However, various leaders were taken, such as Zedekiah, the son of Maaseiah, and Kolaiah, whose son Ahab would later earn further condemnation from God even while he was in captivity.[145] Ahikam the son of Shaphan was not taken, which was a surprise to me, but he had been quite sick for some time, so maybe in his weakened state he had not seemed likely to be any threat to Nebuchadnezzar's plans.

Some of the other captives were people whom I have already mentioned in this diary. One was Benaiah, the son of Kenan, one of the leading men of Anathoth, who had tried to punish me for my attack on an idol back in the eighteenth year of King Josiah. Since that time, he had periodically tried to get me into trouble, but it had never been successful, and now he was quite an old man. He had taken refuge in Jerusalem as Nebuchadnezzar advanced and had been taken into custody when Nebuchadnezzar's commanders ordered a complete listing of all of the people found in the city. My erstwhile friend Benaiah had also been taken, along with some of the others who had been involved in plots to kill me, and had continued to cause trouble for me in Anathoth whenever they could. Fortunately, God had warned me of the worst of their plots and had frustrated several others.

Immer had died in the looting and bloodletting that had followed the capitulation of King Jehoiakim, but his son Pashhur had been taken into captivity exactly as God had foretold when Pashhur had released me from the stocks a day after beating me.

---

[145] Jeremiah 29:21-23

God keeps his promises, and Pashhur suffered as promised.

These details also came from Ishi, Immer's servant, who had gone to tell Pashhur that Immer his father had been killed by the Chaldeans. Ishi told me that there had been no Chaldean soldiers in the temple when he arrived, but that Pashhur had been standing near the gate with a group of other priests, mostly his friends. Ishi had walked toward the group to tell Pashhur about Immer, but as he had approached, he had seen some Chaldean soldiers entering the temple courts, swords unsheathed and shields ready. He told me sheepishly that he had quickly looked for a way to escape, but then decided that the safest place was probably just behind the gatehouse, so he hid there and watched as the group of soldiers approached Pashhur and his cronies. The priests were all unarmed and looked frightened, but Pashhur stepped forward bravely.

"We are priests of Yahweh and this is his holy temple," he announced.

The leader of the soldiers looked at him and spat on the ground in front of him. "Well we are soldiers of Nebuchadnezzar and these are our swords."

The soldiers behind him laughed at his clever reply but the priests looked even more frightened.

"Yahweh's temple is holy and foreigners cannot enter," continued Pashhur boldly.

Some of the priests began to realise that Pashhur's words might be more definite than was wise.

"Your god has had his chance to protect his temple," said the soldier slowly. "If he can't protect it, what chance have you got?"

"You cannot enter," repeated Pashhur, ignoring the raised hands of his friends, who were trying to silence him.

One of his friends said quickly, "Pashhur, maybe you should leave this to us."

The soldier asked in a quiet, sweet voice, "So we are not allowed to enter? You won't let us come in?"

Another of the priests replied ingratiatingly, "We are only priests, not soldiers – we do not get involved with military matters."

But Pashhur's definite voice overrode him, "No, you must not enter."

Pashhur was surrounded now, as his friends braved their fear to do what they could to quiet him. Terror showed in their eyes.

"Pashhur, Pashhur," one said. "Calm down and let us deal with this."

"No, I won't be quiet," protested Pashhur. "This is God's temple and foreigners cannot enter God's house."

"Excuse us sirs," said another of the priests to the soldiers, and his voice was quavering. "We are sorry that this…"

"Silence," shouted the leading soldier. He stepped forward and grabbed the garment of the priest as he spoke. "King Nebuchadnezzar is in charge, and he has given us orders. Resistance means death." He pulled the priest towards him and thrust his sword through his body, then threw him to the ground where he lay in shock as blood poured out, drenching his tunic.

The leader stepped back. "Kill them all," he said, "except the one with the mouth. I want him."

"No," shouted one of the priests, stepping back hurriedly. "It was him who was resisting, not us. Don't kill us! It's his fault."

But the soldiers stepped forward and obeyed their leader's command. Soon all of Passhur's friends lay around him on the stone pavement, dead or dying, and the pavement was covered with their blood.

As Ishi told me these details, the words of God glowed in my mind:

> "The Lord does not call your name Pashhur,
> but *Terror on Every Side.*
> For thus says the Lord:
> Behold, I will make you a terror to yourself
> and to all your friends.
> They shall fall by the sword of their enemies
> while you look on."[146]

My throat constricted and a mixture of terror and utter humility spread over me. God's words had been fulfilled so exactly. How could I be close to a God who was so powerful and holy? And how could my nation survive? God had promised unimaginable destruction – if Yahweh was to fulfil all of his prophecies in such complete detail, who would be left?

Ishi, however, had still more to tell, and reported how Pashhur had been left untouched in his terror, as he stood encircled by the dead bodies of his friends. The leader looked at him and said, "This is what your friends get. I wouldn't want a friend like you. Now, take us to your home."

"No! I'm not telling you where my family is so that you can kill them too. Just kill me."

"Oh, no. We're not going to kill your family – unless you refuse to take us to your house. If you won't take us there, then we will kill you, but be sure that we will also find your house and kill all of your family, one by one."

"How can I know you are telling the truth?" begged Pashhur.

"You can't. You'll just have to trust me."

---

[146] Jeremiah 20:3-4

Pashhur pleaded with the soldier, but he was implacable, and finally Pashhur had to give in.

"I'll lead you there."

"Good," replied the soldier. "As I said, we won't kill them, but you and all of them will come with us to Babylon. And you won't ever be coming back."

Ishi finished his story then, and once again I had the spine-chilling feeling that this was the invisible hand of Yahweh, working as a scribe might work to decorate a scroll in minute, exact detail. The words God had spoken to Pashhur through me had been:

"And you, Pashhur, and all who dwell in your house,
shall go into captivity.
To Babylon you shall go, and there you shall die,
and there you shall be buried,
you and all your friends,
to whom you have prophesied falsely."[147]

Pashhur went into captivity with his entire family, one of very few families to do so when Nebuchadnezzar first took away some of the people of Judah.

ↄʘ

Nebuchadnezzar's advisors had also suggested that it would be best to take away the young men who might cause trouble in the future. Nebuchadnezzar took their advice.

Apparently, he demanded the schooling results from across Judah and Israel and took all the top students with him back to Babylon. Sadly for Shobai and Maacah, that included their son Mishael, whom Shobai had so proudly announced to be the "best student in Bethel". He must have been right.

---

[147] Jeremiah 20:6

Some of the top students won deportation two different ways. Nebuchadnezzar took many of the sons of the nobles, and Zaccai and Abigail's son Daniel was included in that list. But as he also appeared at the very top of the list of students in Jerusalem, either way he would have been leaving his home never to return. He had three friends who went with him though: Hananiah, Mishael and Azariah, who were also outstanding students and were developing a godliness that seemed genuine amongst the deceptive and disobedient religion that filled Jerusalem.

Zaccai and Abigail had lost their only son, and Nebuchadnezzar then proceeded to make sure that none of these young men would ever raise up children to rebel against Babylon. It was just as God had predicted to an earlier king, Hezekiah, about a hundred years before.[148] Hezekiah hadn't worried much about the prediction because he knew it wouldn't be in his time, but the targets of the fulfilment of the prophecy couldn't dismiss it quite so blithely.

Many were led away from Jerusalem bound with heavy chains, suffering as many beatings as it took to convince them to obey whatever instructions they were given.

❧

As Nebuchadnezzar's advisors chose who would stay in Jerusalem and who would be taken to Babylon, Nebuchadnezzar led his army south to make a lightning-fast attack on Egypt. His intention was to push home the advantage he had gained in the Battle of Carchemish and its aftermath.

---

[148] Isaiah 39:5-8

The plan failed. Neco won the battle and Nebuchadnezzar had to withdraw in a certain amount of confusion. He would try again later. In the meantime, he thought it best to return quickly to Babylon to tidy up some more loose ends.

℃

As I turned towards home again, I began to hear in each town I passed through, news of the terrible events that had shaken Jerusalem.

Once I entered Judah, tales of horror were to be heard everywhere, and the stench of rotting corpses enveloped me as I approached Jerusalem.[149] Many men had been given the task of collecting bodies and burying them, but Nebuchadnezzar's army had killed large numbers over a huge area, and some places had few left to bury the dead.

Not only that, but there had been no rain since Nebuchadnezzar had attacked and the land was drying out. Trees were dying and fruit was scarce. Disaster was following disaster, just as God had warned. If only my people had listened!

It was a horrible time as I came to Jerusalem that day. The news had prepared me for tragedy, but Nebuchadnezzar's minor show of strength had gone far beyond my worst imaginings. Many of my friends were dead or deported, and it would be quite some time before I knew who had died and who had been taken away, never to return.

God's word in my mouth had proved true but vindication had never tasted so bitter.

---

[149] Jeremiah 14:18

Chapter 17

A scroll of God's words

I was back in Jerusalem, but the character of the city had subtly changed since I had left. Defeat and death had sapped the people's confidence, and many of the brightest minds and best leaders had gone.

Jehoiakim was still king, but even he seemed a little different. He had only become king at the behest of Pharaoh Neco, but he had then been given considerable freedom, which he had used to establish himself as a king who did what he wanted, when he wanted, and cared little about anyone else. Now he seemed more constrained, as if he had to do what he was told – and didn't like it at all. He still often did just what he wanted, but now he seemed to do it in a more underhanded manner with no discussion. Even more than earlier in his reign, he listened to no-one.

Baruch had been working hard on writing out God's words to me, interrupted only by the Chaldean invasion, which had slowed the work considerably. By the time I returned, it was clear that it wouldn't be finished until the following year, although a lot of the work had been done. Not only that, but he had found some of my writing harder to decipher than the parts he had first looked at. It seemed that my writing was getting worse and worse as I got older! More dictation was found to be necessary, which slowed down the work even more.

During the fifth year of Jehoiakim, Baruch continued his copying and writing from my dictation, and I hoped that we might be ready by the seventh month, the Day of Atonement. As a day of fasting, it would have been a perfect opportunity to obey God's instructions and read his words in the ears of all the people. As it happened, the work was not finished by then, but few people came anyway. King Jehoiakim was not interested in anything that involved fasting or any suggestion that he was in need of forgiveness, and many of the people who would have been driving forces in religious opinions had been removed from the city. Most of the country folk were having to work very hard, doing their best to scratch together some sort of living from their year's work, in the face of the famine that had spread throughout the land. They had no time to spare for religion.

With the passing of the Day of Atonement, I wondered when the reading of God's words would be possible. Would it have to wait for another year – another Day of Atonement?

Finally, in the eighth month, Baruch finished his mammoth task, and soon after, I had finished checking that it was all correct. The work was done, the scroll ready – now we had to wait for a fast day on which to present it to the people.

It was at about that time that we heard the news about the two Benaiahs who had been carried away by Nebuchadnezzar.

Benaiah the son of Kish, my former friend, and his uncle, Benaiah the son of Kenan, had both suffered and walked in chains most of the way to Babylon. Then, at one place where they had stopped for water, something had happened – no-one knew quite what – and the Chaldean soldiers had killed them both. When I heard the news, my mind went immediately to the words of God, spoken after he had warned me about a plot to kill me, made by these very men of Anathoth:

"…therefore thus says the Lord of hosts:
'Behold, I will punish them.
The young men shall die by the sword,
their sons and their daughters shall die by famine,
and none of them shall be left.
For I will bring disaster upon the men of Anathoth,
the year of their punishment.' "[150]

God's vengeance was continuing. Maybe it was working through the worst offenders, or maybe it was just that these were the only victims I had heard much about. I had asked to see God's vengeance upon them,[151] but in his love he had not *shown* me that. Had he made sure that I heard about it though?

❧

It was a big surprise to me when God used the famine to provide us with a fast day on which to read the scroll. The people were really struggling. Food was hard to find because of the destruction that Nebuchadnezzar's army had wreaked on the crops and fruit trees. All the stored

---

[150] Jeremiah 11:22-23
[151] Jeremiah 11:20

provisions had been consumed in the months that followed, but by then the famine had also taken a hand in the disaster. The crops that had been sown after the Chaldean invasion had not produced the increase needed, and famine was destroying the nation.

I have mentioned before that many in Judah considered Yahweh as a god of last resort. People would turn to him when all else failed, but only after trying all the other gods – as if they were trying all the weapons in an arsenal one by one, leaving the least popular weapon until last. All year, the nation had been praying and begging dead idols to listen to their requests, but, naturally, nothing had happened. Now, desperation was in the air, and people began to consider turning to Yahweh.

Normally, the eighth month was a time of cold, rainy weather, but this year was different. The cold had come alright, but the rain had not.

In their wretchedness, the nobles and people of Judah proposed a day of fasting and dedication to Yahweh to beg for his help in the time of famine that was crippling the nation. King Jehoiakim and the priests agreed, and a date was fixed in the ninth month. Word was passed around throughout the length and breadth of Judah, calling the people to Jerusalem for a day of fasting.

I'm not sure what would have happened if the drought and famine had broken before the day of fasting arrived. The timing was such that sowing would normally have been completed by that time, but many had decided not to sow or had nothing that they could sow anyway. If rain – soaking, saturating, streaming rain – had come, would the populace have attended the agreed day of fasting? I cannot tell for sure, but I suspect that those who had delayed or forgone their sowing would have begun sowing immediately, and therefore been far too busy to attend. In that case, God might have been thanked for the reprieve, but probably not.

Sometimes I feel so cynical about my people, and my pessimistic and defeatist attitudes are so much at variance with the happiness and joy I would like to feel about them. Should I be more optimistic? I don't know. All I can say is that my pessimism is normally proved right whenever it can be tested.

In the event, there was no rain, and the day of fasting duly came. Baruch took the scroll and read it in the Lord's house. A long job, and a brave one.

I had asked Gemariah, the brother of Ahikam the son of Shaphan, for permission to use a chamber that he controlled, inside the upper court of the temple, right near the New Gate. Standing there, Baruch would be able to speak to all those who went in or out, or stopped to listen, without a crowd jostling or knocking him.

As soon as the temple gates opened, Baruch was in position, ready to read the scroll. The scroll contained all of the words that God had spoken to me since the thirteenth year of King Josiah, and included all of the messages to Judah, Israel and the surrounding nations.

Baruch was quite tall and had a firm, clear voice which would be easy for anyone to hear who wanted to. I had planned to be there listening, but Baruch and I had discussed it and he had suggested that I should stay away. God had specifically said that he should read it, and, if history was anything to go by, a new face had a better chance of survival than an old face that God's enemies already knew too well.

So I was not there as Baruch began his reading and spoke the words of God to his audience, some of whom could not even have been born when God had first spoken the words to me. One of these young men was Micaiah the son of Gemariah, and the message made such an impression on him that he stayed until the very end of the reading, listening to every word, and then went to tell someone in authority. He went down to the king's house, to the chamber of the secretary where his grandfather had worked as secretary to King Josiah. Various officials were scattered around the room, including his father Gemariah and the then-current secretary, Elishama. All in all, there were about 15 or 20 officials there discussing the situation regarding the famine and the economy, and they all listened while Micaiah reported what he remembered of the words he had heard from Baruch as he read the scroll to the people.

Why is it that just sometimes people will listen, when most of the time they won't? All of these men were old enough to have heard at least some of these words before, but my speaking of the words had never got much response – except for the occasional heated responses from the priests and the people. True, Ahikam and others had once responded to protect me when the people wanted to kill me for words I had spoken against the temple, but there had never been a positive response.

Well, this time there was a bit more of a response, and a positive one at that. The officials sent Jehudi the son of Nethaniah to talk to Baruch. When he arrived, Baruch was still in the same room near the gate of the temple, relaxing after several strenuous hours of reading.

"Bring the scroll that you read in the hearing of the people," said Jehudi, "and come with me."

Of course, this instruction made Baruch rather concerned, knowing what had happened to me on various occasions because of these words, but Jehudi was able to reassure him that the officials did not seem to be angry with him. So Baruch plucked up his courage and accompanied Jehudi to the king's house and into the secretary's room.

When he arrived, the officials welcomed him and asked him to sit down and read the scroll to them. So Baruch read it all over again.

All that time, I was anxiously waiting for Baruch to return to the place where I had been keeping under cover. As I did not know what was happening, it was a worrying time. I kept praying that Baruch would be kept safe and that he had not suffered the same fate as Uriah!

Baruch told me later that he was utterly exhausted by the time he finished his second reading, but it seemed as if it had been worth it because when the officials turned to each other he could see fear in their eyes. They had listened and understood!

After very little conversation, they agreed that they had to report all these words to the king. Naturally – at least, I thought it was natural – Baruch began to feel afraid. Jehoiakim had killed so many people that possessing and reading a scroll which condemned many of his actions was enough to make anyone afraid.

Amazingly enough, at that time the officials were willing to take the risk of passing on the message to the king. It really was a brave thing to do. But for Baruch to have gone to the king himself would have been more than brave – it would have been foolhardy. Of course, if God had said that he should, that would have been a different matter, but he hadn't.

I believe that it was Elnathan the son of Achbor who asked Baruch, "Tell us, please, how did you write all these words? Was it at Jeremiah's dictation?"

Baruch answered them, "Yes, he dictated all these words to me, while I wrote them with ink on the scroll."

When I heard this later, I was glad that I had not been there, because apparently when he gave them that answer, the officials looked at each other and lost some of their enthusiasm for the task. They must have been afraid that having me associated with these words took away some of their power. However, I was even more pleased that they advised Baruch, "Go and hide, you and Jeremiah, and let no one know where you are."

If they had not warned Baruch, he would have been easy to find, and I would have felt very guilty to have had his death on my conscience.

🙰

We heard later from a most apologetic Gemariah what had happened when he and the other officials went into the court to speak to the king. They had left the scroll in the secretary's room for safekeeping, merely reporting its words to the king.

As part of the report, though, someone had mentioned that the words were all written on a scroll. Jehoiakim had seized on that admission and sent Jehudi to get the scroll at once. When he returned with the scroll, Jehoiakim had commanded him to read it aloud. He did so, trying to ignore the king's special sidekicks, who stood around listening and sneering.

"You're not going to like this," Gemariah said as he got to this part of the story, and he looked at Baruch and me sympathetically. "You know that it has been rather cold? Well, King Jehoiakim had a small fire in a brazier in his winter rooms. When Jehudi had read three or four columns, Jehoiakim grabbed the scroll from him and cut off the part that he had read. And do you know what he did with it?"

"No, I have no idea," I replied.

"He threw it into the fire and burned it up."

I was quite shocked at the time, but I shouldn't have been. I looked at Baruch and said, "I'm sorry, Baruch."

"But what about the rest of the scroll?" asked Baruch.

"The whole thing was fed to the fire, piece by piece," said Gemariah. "We tried to get him to stop: Elnathan, Delaiah and I, all of us. But he wouldn't listen and he kept cutting it up as Jehudi read until Jehudi had finished reading the very last piece. Then he threw that piece into the fire as well, and it was all gone. I'm sorry. We tried to stop him."

"Thanks for trying, Gemariah," said Baruch. "It was brave of you. I hope the king won't retaliate or punish you in any way."

"So do we," admitted Gemariah, glumly. "But it seems that he probably won't. It was a bit frightening when he looked at us and called Jerahmeel his son and a pair of his special servants. I really did wonder whether we had gone too far. But he didn't say anything about us. Instead, he told them to go and look for you two."

Baruch and I had been hiding as the officials had recommended, but it had been a very thorough search. We had heard the search from where we were hidden in the temple: shouting, the stamping of feet and banging on doors. In the end, there must have been lots of people looking for us. Hiding inside a room with the door locked, we had kept quiet and ignored both the occasional knocks and the shouts to "Open up!" When someone had finally fetched a key and opened the door, the soldiers who came in had just looked around quickly and left, locking the door again behind them. We had been standing, praying, behind a screen at the back of the room. There was nothing else in the room except one table. Even a cursory search would have found us, but it didn't. God had hidden us from them.

☙

Months of work had gone up in smoke, and both Baruch and I were rather depressed about it. Neither of us wanted to do the work again, but we both wondered whether we should. Just a few days later, God spoke to me again:

"Take another scroll and write on it
all the former words that were in the first scroll,
which Jehoiakim the king of Judah has burned."[152]

I went and purchased a scroll, which was no small amount of money in itself, but the months of work that Baruch must now do again would be the real cost. I was having more and more difficulty finding any spare money, as the famine continued and the number of poor who needed help grew. Still, if God wanted it to happen, he would provide the money, and the ability to do the work. The scroll was delivered to Baruch and he began the work of writing the words of God once more. Slowly, all of the same words were written out again, and then, over time, many more words were added as God continued to speak to me.

At the same time, God also gave me the most damning words for this evil king of Judah:

"Therefore thus says the Lord
concerning Jehoiakim king of Judah:
He shall have none to sit on the throne of David,
and his dead body shall be cast out
to the heat by day and the frost by night.
And I will punish him and his offspring
and his servants for their iniquity.
I will bring upon them
and upon the inhabitants of Jerusalem
and upon the people of Judah
all the disaster that I have pronounced against them,
but they would not hear."[153]

---

152 Jeremiah 36:28
153 Jeremiah 36:30-31

Chapter 18

A new loincloth

April, 600 BC – the 9th year of King Jehoiakim

"Why should we listen to you, Jeremiah?" It was my brother Gemariah speaking, and his tone was bitter.

"It's not listening to me, Gemariah," I replied urgently. "It's listening to Yahweh."

"Oh, 'listening to Yahweh'," he said scornfully. "The words are coming from your mouth. You criticise your family, your town, your nation and even God's temple. But nothing ever happens. Where is the disaster you have said so much about?"

"Nebuchadnezzar came, didn't he?"

"Nations come and nations go – we can expect some trouble from time to time, but you were promising far worse things than that. Where are they?"

"Yahweh is a patient God. When he made his promises to Abraham he said that the sins of the Amorites were not yet complete, and then he waited hundreds of years before he let our fathers enter the land and take over.

He is being patient with us too, but his patience is running out."

"Look, Jeremiah, I have done the best I can to listen to you and be fair. You can call it patience if you want, but how can I keep believing you when I'm still waiting for the fulfilment of things you predicted more than twenty-five years ago?"

"Please just think about one of the things God said through me, Gemariah," I begged. "Do you remember the words:

> " 'you say, "I am innocent;
> surely his anger has turned from me."
> Behold, I will bring you to judgment
> for saying, "I have not sinned."
> How much you go about, changing your way!
> You shall be put to shame by Egypt
> as you were put to shame by Assyria.'[154]

"Ever since the days of Hezekiah, and even earlier, we have turned to Assyria whenever we could, and they have often put us to shame. Then it was Egypt who put us to shame in the battle when Josiah was killed, and gave us the king who is still a shame to us. That prophecy has been fulfilled. Not only that, but King Jehoiakim broke his promise and rebelled against King Nebuchadnezzar two years ago, and we will have to face his wrath again sometime soon."[155]

"A bit too vague for my liking, little brother."

It definitely wasn't an agreement from Gemariah, but at least it was the first time in many years that he had used his old pet name for me.

"Would you prefer God not to be patient? For him to have destroyed Israel during Solomon's reign when he

---

[154] Jeremiah 2:35-36
[155] See 2 Kings 24:1.

abandoned God and followed his wives' gods instead? God is patient. You can't change that."

"If God is so patient, why did first Hasshub and then Hananiah die? Both of our sons taken so early. Where was God's patience for me?"

The pain in my brother's voice showed me again the human side of the suffering that sin brings. For a moment he looked at me, and it may have been the sympathy that he saw in my eyes that made him unable to control himself. He dropped his face into his hands and sobbed, revealing a grief that was still painfully fresh, even after fifteen years.

Whether it be national sin or personal sin, evil brings suffering to everyone, and my brother had suffered from the fulfilment of God's prophecies brought on by sin.

I put my arm around his shoulders and wished that I could heal his hurt. I wondered whether I should respond to his question. Should I tell him of the words that God had spoken to me that might be the start of an answer to his question? God had said to me:

> "You shall not take a wife,
> nor shall you have sons or daughters in this place.
> For thus says the Lord concerning the sons
> and daughters who are born in this place,
> and concerning the mothers who bore them
> and the fathers who fathered them in this land:
> They shall die of deadly diseases.
> They shall not be lamented, nor shall they be buried.
> They shall be as dung on the surface of the ground.
> They shall perish by the sword and by famine,
> and their dead bodies shall be food
> for the birds of the air and for the beasts of the earth."[156]

---

[156] Jeremiah 16:2-4

I had been forbidden to marry because of the sin of my nation and God's patient desire to call them to repentance. My brother had married and had suffered what was only the start of God's promised punishment. Gemariah and Abigail had not suffered as gravely as would others when the promised destruction came fully. Their sons had been mourned and buried, but many children and their parents would be neither mourned nor buried. Bodies would be left to rot where they fell, or thrown into the Valley of Slaughter with countless others.

After a short time, Gemariah controlled his grief and we stood together, just for a little while, as two brothers sharing the afflictions that are part of life. Gemariah mourning his loss, and I feeling for his suffering, but knowing that this was but the start of the outpouring of God's fury on an unrepentant nation.

I decided not to tell him God's words just then. I would find an opportunity later.

℃℞

My brother Gemariah was probably an example of one of the better people of Judah and Jerusalem. Amongst the priests, he held more firmly than most to the worship of only one god. But he felt that life had treated him cruelly, as he and Abigail had been left without any sons or daughters. His work in the temple kept him busy, but we had spoken about God's plans from time to time. I'm sure that he wanted to listen, but he knew how unpopular God's word had made me, and he could not have accepted that easily. As the High Priest's brother, he had a position of importance supervising the Levites, and it was best to stay quiet if you wished to remain on the good side of the priestly hierarchy. He did not want to risk the alienation I had to endure.

Jehoiakim was a cruel and violent king. Arbitrary and selfish, his decisions were often made in the heat of the moment, and friends could become enemies with only one careless sentence. Under his rulership, the city was full of careful people. The rich were mostly insulated from the difficulties of the nation, but the poor suffered greatly – as they normally do.

Jehoiakim left the worship of God largely intact, but gave it no support. Azariah was allowed to continue on as High Priest, and the priests and Levites still stayed busy around the temple, but the king's attention was given to other gods, and people who sought to please the king followed his example. In such a situation, it would have required a stronger and more godly man than Azariah to hold faithfully to the worship that God had commanded.

Instead, Azariah allowed the worship of Yahweh to be tainted by the practices of other religions in a bid for popularity, and the riches that came with it.

The last four years had been difficult times, although the drought had slowly receded after Jehoiakim's fifth year. Unfortunately for the priests and prophets, the recovery had not been dramatic enough for them to be able to claim that Yahweh had seen their fasting and blessed the land as a result. In fact, it had all been rather unsatisfactory for them. Prophets who had prophesied glorious soaking rains and lush growth from Dan to Beersheba had been forced to re-issue their over-enthusiastic proclamations, or just hope that people would be willing to interpret their prophecies to fit with the slight improvement actually observed.

The priests felt the pinch of the reduced offerings and gifts, and stooped to blackmail and extortion to restore their income. God's temple was very much a safe haven for robbers.

News from the captives who had been taken to Babylon came only rarely. The best news I heard was from Zaccai, who had received a letter from his son Daniel reporting that he and his friends had been blessed amazingly in their Chaldean education and now occupied positions in Nebuchadnezzar's court and across the province of Babylon. He had even written about a breathtaking miracle that had saved his friends from a furnace in which they were to have been executed. But that was really all the good news we heard. Apart from them, the captives were being allowed to settle in Babylon, but learning to live in a pagan society is not easy for any who care about Yahweh, the God of Israel.

❧

Later in the ninth year of Jehoiakim, God gave me what seemed a very strange instruction. I was in Anathoth at the time, in my mother's home, still working on the project that had occupied my spare time for many years – reviewing and categorising the scrolls of religious writings. I don't remember what I was reading at the time, but suddenly I felt God's presence again, for the first time in several months. Burning, shocking, frightening, but as welcome as a meal to a starving man, the spirit of God was flaming within me. Suddenly a whisper enveloped me, almost silent, although it felt like the searing stab of a white-hot blade. Yahweh breathed:

> "Go and buy a linen loincloth
> and put it around your waist,
> and do not dip it in water."[157]

Immediately the voice was gone and I was alone again, feeling a little dazed. Standing up, I walked to the door and opened it, absently making sure that I had some

---

[157] Jeremiah 13:1

money with me. As I opened the door, my mother was standing there, obviously about to knock or call out.

"What happened, Jeremiah?" she asked, concerned. "I heard a sound."

"God spoke to me. But it was just a whisper – what did you hear?"

"I heard… I can't really say what," said my mother uncertainly. "It was almost as if a wind had come into the house somehow. Quiet, but somehow firm. Was that the presence of God?"

"I don't know exactly what you heard, but the presence of God was certainly here. His whisper gave me an instruction, and now I must go and obey. I must buy a loincloth."

God's urgency was upon me, so I walked swiftly from the house to look for Elkanah, the local draper and tailor who sold such cloths along with a wide range of other items. He often walked around the houses of Anathoth at various times of day, calling out, in a piercing, high-pitched voice, the nature and value of his wares. God's instruction had come before there was any sound of his voice echoing in Anathoth, yet I found him almost immediately, just as he was about to start his circuit of the town. Quickly, I described my needs, and then selected a cloth from the pile he offered me. He named the price and looked a little disappointed as I paid without haggling. I had got a loincloth as God had instructed. Normally, I would have given the cloth a quick wash before using it, but God's words had been clear, so I went back to the house and put it on straight away.

Of course, an urgency to act was one thing and I had done it, but my curiosity was quite another. Why did God want me to do such a strange thing? Surely I would hear more about this from God very soon?

Years of experience in listening to the words of God had left me confident, yet uncertain. Confident that God would speak again soon, but uncertain as to when "soon" might be.

I didn't know quite what to do next, so I decided to return to my work in the scroll room, but as I reached the door, my mother called to me, "Jeremiah, did you get the cloth you needed?"

"Yes, mother. Of course," I said, turning to her as she entered the main room where I stood.

"And I suppose it took you quite a while to find Elkanah?"

"Mother, you know it can't have taken a long time. I am back very quickly."

"I suppose that's my point, Jeremiah. God told you to do something and chose exactly the right time to tell you for it to happen quickly."

"Yes, mother. It normally works like that."

"You are blessed... so very blessed. Blessed even when he gives you difficult assignments. You have the word of the creator in your ears. The work of the creator in your hands. The presence of the creator around you and within you."

"You're right, mother. And I am happy to do God's work – but sometimes it is very hard and I would almost prefer him to send someone else. It is hard to be hated."

"God has been hated for much longer than you, my son," my mother said, stopping and smiling for a moment, before continuing, "...and ignored. And misquoted. And misunderstood. Small wonder that the same happens to his prophets."

"Yes, I understand that, but..." I heaved a sigh, "twenty-seven years, mother. That's how long I have been taking his words to the people, and there is still so little to show for it. I can't complain about God's patience, but it makes my job even harder. People hear my words and wait for them to be fulfilled, but twenty-seven years is too long for them to wait. Two weeks is the sort of time period they understand," I finished, bitterly.

"It will happen in God's good time. And anyway, hoping for disaster to come more quickly is not really very sensible. Have you ever wondered what will happen to you or me at that time?"

Of course I had, but I had no answer, nothing to either comfort or terrify. God's words to me concentrated on other things.

As I thought of this, I again heard and felt the presence of God. Quickly, I opened the door to the scroll room and hurried inside, hoping that my mother would understand.

Inside the scroll room, the presence of God enveloped me once more, and again the whisper seemed to cut through me:

> "Take the loincloth that you have bought,
>   which is around your waist, and arise,
>   go to the Euphrates and hide it there
>   in a cleft of the rock."[158]

That was all. The whisper passed and the presence of God released its grip upon me.

I had to go, immediately, but I would have some questions to keep me company on the journey: was I still glad to hear the voice of God? Was I still glad to do the work of God?

---

[158] Jeremiah 13:4

It took more than two long, hard weeks of walking to get to the Euphrates River. By that time, the loincloth was not feeling very new any more – nor very clean, either.

After reaching the Euphrates, it took me another two days to find a place where I could follow God's command about putting the loincloth "in a cleft of the rock". Finally, I found a place away from any towns – a place where there was a cleft of the rock down near the river. It was an ideal place to hide something that must be found again, and I had a nagging feeling that I would need to do so, although God had not said so explicitly.

Clambering down into the fissure I had found, I took off the loincloth and buried it in the sandy gravel that formed a tiny little beach at the water's edge between the two rocky sides of the cleft. In that quiet and lonely place, I was also able to take a much-needed bath in the Euphrates River and to sit in prayer thanking God for his care in leading me safely to my destination and guiding me in his work. My meditations on my journey had confirmed once again that hearing the voice of God was a delight to me, and that doing his work – even when it hurt me – was a joy. I was still glad to be his prophet, despite twenty-seven years of being alternately harassed and ignored. The terrifying pleasure of the presence of God always outweighed anything else.

"What now?" I asked myself, once my prayer of thanks was finished. I was far enough north that it seemed sensible to visit some of the kings of the north that God had instructed me to warn regarding the cup of his wrath. Did God want me to do so?

I spent two days there, near the cleft, walking to and fro beside the river as I prayed and asked God for guidance. Although I did not realise it at the time, my walking was making me more familiar with the bank of the Euphrates in that area, learning its folds and headlands, its bays and inlets. This familiarity was to prove very helpful later on, when I needed to find my hidden loincloth again.

After two days, I was given the answer I needed and set off, heading even further north. I entered areas I had never visited before, carrying a message that none of its recipients wanted. Yet again, God was stretching my faith and testing my endurance. But throughout the journey, he was close by my side, just as I needed him to be.

October, 599 BC – the 11th year of King Jehoiakim

More than a year passed before I eventually returned to Judah. At that time Jehoiakim had just begun the eleventh year of his reign, and he was not improving as a king. People continued to die at his command, and the blood of the innocent poor stained both the corridors of his palace and the streets of Jerusalem.

One day, the word of Yahweh came to me, and his voice pulsated with more anger than I had ever felt before:

"Thus says the Lord concerning Jehoiakim
the son of Josiah, king of Judah:
'They shall not lament for him, saying,
"Ah, my brother!" or "Ah, sister!"
They shall not lament for him, saying,
"Ah, lord!" or "Ah, his majesty!"
With the burial of a donkey he shall be buried,
dragged and dumped
beyond the gates of Jerusalem.' "[159]

As God's voice faded, I rejoiced at his words. Jehoiakim deserved all that God had promised him, and

---

[159] Jeremiah 22:18-19

the sooner it happened, the fewer innocent lives would be taken. It couldn't happen too soon for me.

All I wanted to know was exactly how this magnificent judgement would occur. Would I be able to see God's punishment on this evil man? But God's planning was to mean that I missed this key event also.

ↄↃ

August, 598 BC – the 11th year of King Jehoiakim

> "Arise, go to the Euphrates,
> and take from there the loincloth
> that I commanded you to hide there."[160]

With these words, God dispatched me on another long journey north. As I travelled, I heard news from other wayfarers; warnings of an army. King Nebuchadnezzar of Babylon was on the move again, and the rumours suggested that he was heading for Jerusalem.

Crossing to the coast, I hurried on, moving as quickly as I could until I had passed the danger zone. After that, I travelled inland until I reached the Euphrates, where I hunted for the particular cleft in the rocky riverside that I sought. After almost two years, it was not easy to find, for wind, rain and floods all leave their mark on the land and subtly change its appearance.

Eventually, though, I was confident that I had found the right site. Quickly, I climbed down into the fissure and dug in its sandy floor until I uncovered a ragged and rotting piece of material. It had to be the loincloth that I had hidden there – it could be nothing else – but it was utterly ruined. As I held the cloth in my hand and saw its tattered holes and tears, the word of the Lord came to me:

---

[160] Jeremiah 13:6

A new loincloth

"Thus says the Lord:
Even so will I spoil the pride of Judah
and the great pride of Jerusalem.
This evil people, who refuse to hear my words,
who stubbornly follow their own heart
and have gone after other gods
to serve them and worship them,
shall be like this loincloth, which is good for nothing.
For as the loincloth clings to the waist of a man,
so I made the whole house of Israel
and the whole house of Judah cling to me,
declares the Lord, that they might be for me a people,
a name, a praise, and a glory,
but they would not listen."[161]

God also spoke many other words, but I spent little time thinking about them at the time. I was in a hurry to get home. What would I find when I reached Jerusalem?

Had King Nebuchadnezzar really attacked Judah? And if he had, would this be the end for King Jehoiakim?

---

[161] Jeremiah 13:9-11

Free Download

Paul in Snippets

A 109-page PDF novelette by Mark Morgan.

The life of Paul painted from the Acts of the Apostles.

Get your free copy of *Paul in Snippets* when you sign up for the Bible Tales mailing list. As well as the eBook, you will receive a weekly email newsletter with micro tales, informative articles and special offers.

Visit **http://www.BibleTales.online/free-pins**

www.BibleTales.online

Bible Tales Online

Other books by Mark Morgan are available from Bible Tales Online.

Terror on Every Side!

THE LIFE OF JEREMIAH

From a family of priests in the peaceful reign of good King Josiah, came a young man Jeremiah, bringing words from God to his people. It was no message for the fainthearted, either. It was a message of *Terror on Every Side!*

Volume 1 – Early Days
Volume 2 – As Good As It Gets
Volume 3 – Darkness Falling
Volume 4 – The Darkness Deepens
Volume 5 – No Remedy

Generally available as paperback, eBook and audiobook.

Micro-tales

Collections of short stories about Bible characters or events, available in paperback, eBook and audiobook.

Fiction Favours the Facts
Fiction Favours the Facts – Book 2

Other novels

Joseph, Rachel's son

Bible Tales Online continues to publish books.
To find the list of currently available books, visit

http://www.BibleTales.online/books

www.BibleTales.online